WAYWARD BOND

MATED TO THE ALIEN UNIVERSE

DETYEN WARRIOR OUTCASTS
BOOK THREE

KATE RUDOLPH

ABOUT THE BOOK

Someone wants to hurt me.

I'm sure of it as soon as I wake up on Nebula Outpost, rescued after ten years of being stranded on a planet full of death and pain.

Without protection, the company responsible for all that suffering will do whatever it takes to silence me.

Zyrus is my protector.

He's stoic and achingly familiar. I've been stranded for a decade, so how can I know him?

His touch is electrifying, but he sacrificed his emotions long before we met. He can't feel anything, least of all desire for me.

So why does fire burn in his eyes every time he's

near me? And how can I unleash the passion I know he has hidden inside of him?

1
ZYRUS

Fun. Freedom.

Females.

After a particularly precarious mission, this leave was what I needed to loosen up and relax. Honora Station wasn't the most exciting place in the galaxy, but it was bustling with life from all corners of the universe, and there were always people looking to get into my kind of trouble.

"If you get arrested, I'm not bailing you out." Kyric sipped his beer and looked at me with a leery grimace.

So, my reputation had gotten around. I laughed and slammed down the rest of my drink before ordering another. Our time here was limited, and I was going to make the most of it. "I'm not going to get arrested."

"Again?" he prompted.

"I wasn't charged." A few hours in a holding cell had been enough to have me bouncing off the walls, about ready to confess to any crime to make it stop. No confession was needed when my eye was swollen from the sucker punch that started the fight, and they let everyone go after we were sufficiently cowed.

"Keep your comm on. We're on leave, but I've been hearing whispers. We could be recalled at any moment." Kyric didn't order a second beer.

Such was life in the Detyen Legion. We scoured the galaxy looking for clues as to who destroyed our planet a hundred years ago and taking care of any evildoers we came across in the meantime.

"Understood, Boss." I stood, taking the newly poured drink with me and leaving Kyric alone in the bar. He'd sip his drink slowly, claiming to savor the flavors, then go for a walk in the flower garden or some boring shit like that. As if he didn't feel the ticking of the clock just as strongly as I did, as if death wasn't coming for both of us, moment by unceasing moment.

I chugged the rest of my drink and set the glass

aside. I was on leave; I wasn't going to spend it moping about the Denya Price or the borrowed time I was living on. I had seven years to find my mate and a whole legion of brothers behind me. Life was good.

But Honora Station was boring.

There were plenty of places to get drunk, but by station time it was still morning, and the seedier ones wouldn't open until nightfall. The station was a mix of permanent residents and travelers, people rushing to and fro, trying to get to connecting flights that would take them anywhere but here. It was like spending leave in a planet-side space port except there were hotel rooms.

But no one was giving me orders. That was something to appreciate.

I ducked into an arcade and wasted fifteen minutes spending my hard-earned credits on games that were obviously rigged. There was no way I couldn't get the ball I was tossing in a single bucket. I was a trained soldier. And I put extra credits in the machine to regain my honor. But before I could spend all my credits on proving myself to an empty arcade, I forced myself to step away.

Not worth it.

I started walking again. I wasn't going

anywhere, but every time I came to a split in the hallway, a choice to go down one concourse or another, I moved without conscious thought, like instinct was guiding me somewhere I didn't know I needed to be.

I ended up in the arrivals terminal, the place teeming with people carrying luggage and rushing to get on with their journeys.

The crowd parted, and a human woman stepped through.

Denya.

The oxygen was sucked out of the room as I tried to take a deep breath. But the only way to get enough was to step closer to her—the source of the air I breathed. The whole universe seemed to shift and realign with that recognition, my soul alight with joy as I recognized my true purpose in one glance.

Her gaze shifted, and our stares connected. She looked at me for a long moment before her lips tugged up into a lopsided smile. She had dark hair that was pulled back, a few strands of it falling in front of her pale face. And as I got closer, again moving without thought, I saw the hint of freckles and the dark brown of her eyes.

She was perfect.

She was everything.

"Good evening," she said, voice low and smooth. Then she shook her head a bit. "Or morning? What time is it? I'm sorry. I've been traveling for a week."

"What time do you want it to be?" I wanted to reach out and touch her, to sweep her into my arms, kiss her, and take her away to someplace quieter where we could get to know one another and seal the bond simmering between us.

"Are you the welcome committee? Because this is stranger than any port I've landed at so far." She paused for a moment. "Good, though. I think. Do I know you?"

"You will." I held out my hand. "Let me show you around the place."

She hesitated. "I have to ... I don't even know your name."

"I'm Zyrus. I can call my friend Kyric if you need a reference." Though Kyric was as likely to tell her the bad over the good. Maybe I wouldn't call him. "What's your name?" I couldn't just call her "mate," could I?

"Astrid."

"There, now you know my name. All good?" Energy buzzed in my veins. If I touched her, I might explode. If I didn't, I'd go mad.

I'd heard of the intensity of the denya bond, but nothing could have prepared me for this. The whole place could be coming down around us, and all I'd care about was Astrid.

Astrid. I let the name roll around my mind like a caress. A perfect name for a perfect mate.

She muttered something I couldn't quite make out and put her hand in mine. I closed my fingers around hers, and everything settled into place. Yes, this was exactly where I was supposed to be.

I lead her out of the arrivals terminal. "Where are you coming from?" I asked. She only had a small bag with her, so either she'd checked her luggage to her final destination, or it was waiting at the baggage claim.

"Kursica. It's a small colony no one's ever heard of. And it's about a trillion light years from anywhere. I'm only halfway through my trip."

Our trip. Or I'd ask her to return to the legion with me. It wasn't desertion when we found our mates; the legion couldn't stop the hand of fate.

Well. Except when it did. But I didn't have to think about the soulless anymore. My mate was right in front of me, and we were going to start our lives together today.

"I've never heard of it." I'd been across a lot of the galaxy, but never there.

"It's an Earth colony, and its failing. Time to move on to greener pastures."

"Are you from Earth?" That place I'd heard of, though again, never been. Not many aliens went there; it was too far out of the way.

"I suppose. What about you?" Her thumb teased my wrist, sending a shiver up my arm. "I've never seen anyone like you before."

"Detyen. But I travel all over the place. No fixed planet." That wasn't exactly true. The Legion had Detyen HQ on a frozen, inhospitable moon, but that wasn't anyone's true home, no matter how long they lived there. It was just a safe place.

Before I could get caught up in the tragedy of my people, I swept Astrid down another hall, following the distant call of music. One of the atriums was full of people swaying to the beat of a small band playing on the stage. I pulled Astrid close. "Dance with me?"

She was already in my arms. We fit together just as fate had intended. Her body molded against mine, soft and yielding. "Zyrus."

"Yes?" Anything she wanted, I'd give her. Anything she needed, I'd provide.

"What are we doing?"

That was easy. "Dancing."

"This feels ... It's like magic." Her fingers teased the back of my neck, playing with the ends of my braid. "But it can't be real."

"It's real." It was a promise, a vow.

I wanted to kiss her. The moment was perfect, the lights dim, the band playing a romantic tune. And she looked up at me with those wide eyes, yearning for more.

I leaned in and covered her lips with my own. She gasped, lips parting, and I swept my tongue in, tasting her. She was sweet, like honey and spice, and I wanted to devour her.

Now.

My body pulsed with desire, need surging through me with every breath. I wanted to claim her right there, to make her mine for the whole galaxy to see. But perhaps a bit of privacy first.

The loudspeaker overhead buzzed an announcement that I couldn't quite make out, and in that same moment, my comm buzzed. I wanted to ignore it. Nothing else mattered when Astrid was right there.

But I had to report this to Kyric, to let him know my status had changed.

My comm buzzed again, and I pulled it out of my pocket, reluctantly pulling away from my mate. "I have to deal with this," I said and shuffled back a few paces to where it was a bit quieter.

Kyric had left a message telling me where my hotel room was for the next few nights and asking whether or not I wanted to get dinner with the rest of the crew on the station.

I had a feeling I'd be busy by dinner time. And good thing I had the hotel room to myself. I turned around, ready to tell Astrid the good news.

But she was gone.

I looked around, thinking she'd just wandered a little way away. I didn't see her. And when I called, she didn't answer.

I tore through the balcony, looking at every person, in every corner, but it was as if she'd disappeared into thin air.

Where was she? Had she been taken? I needed my mate.

I retraced our steps. If she'd walked away, she was only a minute or two ahead of me, but I must have chosen the wrong hallways. I couldn't find my mate.

I searched for hours, for longer than we'd spent together. I went to every gate in the departure terminal, scanned every human face, but none of them were Astrid.

This had to be some terrible mistake.

But I didn't find her that night. Or the next day. Or the next.

When my leave ended, I got on the transport alongside Kyric and headed back to the Legion. But I knew my mate was out there.

And I was going to find her again.

Somehow.

2
ASTRID

11 Years Later - Nebula Outpost

Fingers brushed against my neck, their grip slowly tightening until the flow of air cut off and I couldn't breathe. I struggled against the hold, trying to tear the hand away, but no matter how much I fought, I couldn't get a grip on what had me.

I was going to die.

I struggled even harder as black circles dotted my vision and my lungs burned. I'd come so far, survived so much. I couldn't let some invisible force finally do me in.

My eyes popped open.

A dream.

I batted the edge of the sheet away. It had been brushing against my neck, no doubt triggering the nightmare. I was in my quarters on Nebula Outpost. I was safe.

Ish.

My whole existence here still felt sort of like a dream. For the last ten years, I'd been subsisting down on the planet of Nebula after a mine disaster left us stranded and thought dead. Our only company was a nasty group of criminals who'd tried to enslave me and my fellow survivors and destroy our camp.

For years, I'd thought I would die down there one day, and I nearly had. But now I was in Nebula Outpost, and I got to enjoy luxuries like baths and my bed and regular soap.

I'd never known those were the things I'd yearn for, but it really was life's little luxuries that mattered.

I checked the clock. It was the middle of the night. The station hummed with the noises of the engines that kept us afloat in orbit over Nebula, but just about everyone would be asleep right now.

No one was coming for me. Not right now.

But I'd been sure they would when I woke up in the hospital a week ago. The mine owners had chosen not to search for survivors on Nebula, and it wouldn't look good for them if we started talking. I feared they would send someone to silence me before I could get the rest of my friends off the planet.

Everyone except Alice was still down there, waiting for ships that I had to make sure showed up. I hadn't chosen to leave. I had been unconscious, bleeding out on the ground, and my only chance at survival was a desperate run in a stolen ship back up to Nebula Outpost. But now, it was my life mission to make sure everyone else got rescued.

I settled back down onto my bed and breathed deeply. Everything was fine. It was just a nightmare. I was as safe as I was going to be. I closed my eyes and tried to let sleep engulf me.

I didn't realize I was screaming until the door burst open and *he* looked in.

Zyrus.

The peculiar Detyen who was in charge of keeping me safe.

I clutched my blankets to my chest, breaths heaving in and out. "I'm fine," I said before he could ask.

Zyrus looked at me, expression somehow both blank and intense. He didn't show much emotion. I couldn't get a read on him, but there was something familiar about the guy, something that had been nagging at the back of my mind since the first moment I saw him in the infirmary. He was watching me as a favor to one of his friends, using his hard-earned vacation time to stay with me almost every hour of every day.

No one had tried to hurt me yet. Maybe it was just my own paranoia.

"Was there a threat?" Zyrus asked.

"Just a nightmare." I should have sent him away then. I was a grown woman; I didn't need an overgrown blue teddy bear in my bed to keep me safe.

Definitely not in my bed.

Zyrus had an icy demeanor; nothing about him was inviting. I was pretty sure he didn't fuck. Not that I should be thinking about that at all. I was still recovering from my injuries, he was here to protect me, and I didn't have room in my head for complications.

"Would you like me to sleep in here?" Zyrus asked. There was no change in his intonation, no hint of judgment.

The bed was plenty big, and I scooted to one side to make room. I had spent the last decade sleeping on a salvaged cot from the remnants of the destroyed mine. The bed I had now was almost too spacious.

"I meant the floor," he said.

"There's plenty of room for both of us here. Don't be ridiculous." He hesitated for a moment before sliding in beside me. All I could feel was his body heat, but something in me relaxed at the knowledge that he was right there by my side, keeping me safe.

Still, it was quite a while before I fell asleep.

My quarters seemed spacious when it was just me and Zyrus. When we were joined by Noelle, Ryklin, Drex, Pippa, and Alice, they began to feel a little strained. I liked the luxuries on Nebula Outpost, mostly the hot running water. But I had gotten used to all the space down on Nebula. It was easy to find privacy, easy to run away and hide in the forest for a little bit, only a few feet away from the encampment and yet in a world of one's own.

Nebula Outpost was all cold steel and technology. It had to be. It was a space station in orbit above the planet of Nebula. There was greenery in some of the atriums, but none of it was enough.

I supposed I would get used to it. I had moved

plenty of times in my life before, had found plenty of new homes. This was just one more change.

I didn't know Drex and Pippa very well. I supposed I didn't know Noelle or Ryklin very well either, but they had saved my life and were the reason my people were not going to be stuck on Nebula anymore. I trusted them. Alice was there too, and I'd known her for a decade. Her, I trusted with my life. She'd come with me in the transport ship, using what little medical care she knew to keep me alive until we found a doctor. This was everyone I knew on Nebula Outpost. My whole life condensed into one room. These were the only people I could trust.

I *hoped* I could trust them.

"Have we heard anything about the others?" I asked. There were a hundred or so people down in the encampment. More, maybe, after we'd rescued some people who had been forced to work in the defunct mine. There was plenty of room on the space station, so I didn't know what the holdup was.

"Nothing yet," said Pippa. She made a frustrated face. "I don't know why station security is dragging their feet on this. I swear they would do anything as long as it meant they didn't have to do their actual jobs."

"Is that fair?" Noelle asked. She and Pippa were best friends, had known each other for years, apparently. It was one of those things that was easy to tell just from looking at them.

"You have just as much reason as I do not to trust station security," Pippa responded.

Noelle didn't say anything back to that.

My impressions of station security weren't great either, but I didn't know enough to really make a judgement. Ten years ago, I had arrived at Nebula Outpost and only spent a few hours here before heading down to my job on Nebula. I'd gone through a basic security check, but it hadn't been particularly thorough. Since I'd come back, nothing seemed to have improved.

"My contact in security says they're working on it," said Ryklin. He and Noelle's hands were clasped together.

I glanced over at Zyrus. He had the same expression he always had, but I thought he was looking at me, only for a second. He looked away, as if it was nothing. Maybe his eyes were just taking in all of the room.

"What about the danger?" asked Alice.

"No one has approached me. No one tried to

stop me from contacting my family. I'm not sure anyone wants to hurt us."

My every instinct said that was wrong. Someone had pulled a guard off my room when I was in the hospital wing. Someone had made me vulnerable to an attack. At this point, it would be easy to get rid of me and Alice and hurt anyone down on Nebula. This was the time where they could stop the story of our survival from getting out.

"I will watch Astrid for as long as she needs," said Zyrus.

"What about your shifts? You've only got so much leave time," said Drex.

"I'll watch her for as long as she needs," he repeated.

Alice didn't have a bodyguard. She kept saying she didn't want one. And maybe I was just being paranoid. I should probably tell Zyrus right now that I was fine and he could go back to work and stop worrying about me.

I kept my mouth shut.

The meeting broke up not too long after that. It was almost lunch time, and I was hungry, but I didn't want to stay in my room and eat some sort of prepared meal from the food processor. The main cafeteria was slightly better, and maybe being around people would make me feel better.

Zyrus was my silent shadow as we walked down the hall. I was only a few doors down from where Pippa and Noelle each lived with their partners. We passed my door and kept going toward the cafeteria. In the first day or two, while Zyrus was watching me, I had tried to make small talk. He was bad at it. He answered questions as succinctly as he could, preferably using one word or less. Now, I didn't ask him anything.

We turned another corner down the narrow hall that would feed us into one of the activity hubs of this area of the station. My stomach grumbled. Then the lights went dark, and somebody barreled into me from the side.

3
ZYRUS

THE LIGHTS WENT OUT at the same moment Astrid grunted. Instinct took over, and I sprang into action, getting between Astrid and her attacker and letting loose. I should have been a thing of madness and fury, a man defending his mate.

But I was still soulless. Cold. Logical.

It didn't matter. My fists connected all the same. The attacker was small, not as strong as me, but quick. I blocked a blow to the throat and struck a kidney, but the figure danced away and dived down toward my ankles, as if they could trip me up.

I jumped and kicked out, catching the attacker in the side. They hissed and backed off, and the lights flickered back to life. I reached out to stop them from running, but they tore out of my grasp and were gone before I got a good look.

I was ready to give chase. This person had *dared* to attack my mate. They would pay.

But Astrid made a small sound in the back of her throat, and I froze.

Another man might have ignored it, but I couldn't, not until I was sure Astrid was safe. And no force in the universe could make me leave her side just now.

It should have been emotional. I knew exactly who she was to me. Every night for eleven years I'd replayed our hour together, memorizing every detail, trying to figure out what had gone wrong, why she'd left. Before I sacrificed my soul, it had been a small torture. Afterwards, it didn't hurt to remember, but I made sure to keep it up, to remember my true purpose in life.

That purpose had no idea who I was.

I could see it every time she looked at me. Rather, I couldn't see it. She didn't remember that day on Honora Station. It hadn't recalibrated her entire existence. To her, I was just some alien.

When I had thoughts like that, I was not disappointed that I was still soulless. If I could feel and my mate thought I was nothing, there was no telling what I would do.

But why couldn't I feel her?

Two months ago, I would have said it was a simple fact of existence. But Ryklin and Drex had both found their mates, had somehow healed their minds so that they now felt just as much as anyone. What did I need to do?

Right now, I needed to help my mate, emotions be damned.

I got my arm around her and helped her to her feet. "Are you injured?" I asked. She looked a bit dazed, her hair falling out of its tie and eyes wide in fear.

"Who was that?" Her voice was steady. Even in fear, my mate was solid.

"I couldn't tell. Someone who can punch." My side ached from where they'd landed a lucky shot, but there would be no more damage than a bruise, nothing to be concerned about.

"Are you alright?" She stepped out of my embrace to fully look at me. My body missed her touch.

"Yes. And you?" She didn't appear to need a medic, but she was clutching her hand to her chest. "Let's go back to your quarters so I can look at that."

She made a face I couldn't interpret; it didn't look like something caused by pain. "It's just a cut. I scraped myself on the freaking wall. I can handle it."

"Let me; I have basic first aid training." It was true. It was logical. But that wasn't what was pushing me forward. My mate was injured, however superficially, and it was my responsibility to tend to that.

It was also my responsibility to make sure it didn't happen in the first place. I'd failed on one count, I wouldn't on the second.

Without another word, Astrid walked with me back to her room. The room had once belonged to a woman named Fran who'd been murdered by a Detyen determined to somehow circumvent the Denya Price. Detyens died at the age of thirty unless we found and claimed our mates. Everyone knew that. What they didn't know was the dirty secret of the Detyen Legion.

The soulless.

The Detyen Legion hadn't come up with the technology themselves. It had been discovered in the depths of a data drive, hidden under so many layers of encryption that it had never meant to see the light of day. The Legion may have never tried the procedure, but then Detya was destroyed, and our numbers were decimated. Since then, when a warrior approached his thirtieth year, he was given a choice: die with honor or sacrifice his emotions to remain living and serve the Legion.

It had never been a choice for me. I knew Astrid was out there, and I had to find her.

And then there were the people like me and my fellow ex-warriors who lived on Nebula Outposts. We'd all failed someway, showed some weakness that made the Legion question our right to exist. And we'd each escaped here to avoid a death sentence.

Life was short and brutally regimented for the soulless.

"Sit," I told Astrid once I locked the door to her quarters behind us. I grabbed the first aid kit from the bathroom and knelt at her feet to better tend her wound.

Astrid sucked in a deep breath. I didn't know why. I hadn't touched her yet.

"Give me your hand. Please." I added the last as an afterthought.

She hesitantly held it out, and I turned it palm up. It was a superficial injury. She'd barely bled, but there was a long scrape on her forearm that had torn the skin.

"Does it hurt?" I dabbed a sterile wipe along the wound. Every place my fingers touched her bare skin sent jolts of pain up my own hand, as if I was gripping ice cubes. But I wouldn't let go.

"It's fine." I could tell it was a lie. The skin around her lips was taut, she'd gone a bit pale, and there was a bead of sweat on her brow. That could have been the disinfectant, though. It stung to the deepest hells.

I rubbed a healing cream that contained a numbing agent over the wound and covered that with a bandage. She'd be as good as new in a day or so.

I couldn't let go of her hand. I should have. My body screamed at me that this was wrong, that the pain would only get worse the longer I held on. It was climbing up my arm now, a warning that I refused to heed.

Astrid wasn't pulling away either. Her gaze met mine, eyes boring in deep, as if looking long enough would unlock a puzzle. "Who are you, Zyrus?"

We'd been around one another for a week. She knew perfectly well who I was. That wasn't what she was asking. She wanted to know who I was to *her*.

She didn't remember.

The day we'd met was burned into my memory, the one constant in a life turned upside down more than once. But that day didn't mean the same to her.

I could tell her. Perhaps that would be the wise move. But a stubborn part of me that had survived even through the soulless procedure wanted her to remember me, wanted to see that recognition bloom.

Instead, I flipped her hand over and brushed a kiss against her knuckles.

Pain exploded in my head, and I ignored it all the same. I didn't feel emotion, not even with my mate, but I could feel this, and I had to believe it was proof that something was real between us.

She sucked in a deep breath, and her hand twitched in mine, but she still didn't pull away.

I could kiss her now. I could lean in and cover her lips with my own, taste her as I had once before. Perhaps that would remind the denya bond of who she was to me. Perhaps that would bring my emotions back so that I could claim my mate as I should have more than a decade ago.

I almost leaned in. But the pain in my head grew

even worse until I heard Astrid curse and pull away. She leaned around me to grab a piece of gauze from the first aid kit.

"Your nose is bleeding," she said, holding the gauze in offering.

I took it.

Kissing would have to wait.

4

ASTRID

I was running. I was always running. The walls around me got narrower and narrower, but it did nothing to slow me down. I had to get there.

Had to find him.

I called out, but I couldn't hear the word, the name, that came out of my mouth. It was like my head was muffled by cotton, my mouth completely disconnected. But I had to keep going. Had to find ...

Zyrus.

I jerked up from where I'd dozed off on the couch, the dream trying to claw me back down. My eyes immediately went to Zyrus, who was preparing a drink in the food prep area. He was as quiet as a ghost, and I took a moment to admire the broad planes of his back, covered by his dark shirt but hinting at plenty for my imagination.

My imagination was having a field day with him.

He kept showing up in my dreams, and not the sexy kind, which I would understand. To say it had been a long time since someone had touched me would be an understatement. With only a hundred survivors down on Nebula, the pickings had been slim, and none had appealed, not even in my loneliest night.

There was only ... The memory slipped away before I could grasp it, the same thought that had been nagging at me for weeks.

I was forgetting something important, or at least it felt like I was, like I'd lit a candle and left the house without blowing it out. Not that candles were allowed on Nebula Outpost.

I brushed my thumb over my knuckles, imagining there was some kind of imprint from where Zyrus had brushed his lips against them. I expected there to be a mark, something to prove it had really happened. Those moments while he'd tended to the tiniest of scrapes had washed away the fear of the attack so much that I hadn't actually thought about it.

Zyrus was a distraction. But was that a good thing?

I put my feet flat on the ground, sitting fully up. Zyrus turned around, mug in hand. "Would you like something to drink?" he asked, voice flat, no hint of the man who'd treated me so tenderly.

"No, thanks." I reached for my comm and stared at the screen blankly for a moment before remembering how to turn it on. The tech hadn't changed that much in the last decade, but I was rusty.

No messages from anyone, not that there was anyone who'd be calling me. My family, if any of them were left, was scattered across the galaxy, and I'd written them off long before getting stranded on Nebula. Everyone else that I knew lived just a few doors down in either direction.

"I've been scouring the station's systems to try and figure out who attacked you, but the camera wasn't functioning in that corridor, and the data seems to be wiped for that sector for the fifteen minutes leading up to the attack. Are you certain you don't recall anything else?" Zyrus took a seat across from me and set his mug down on the table.

"It all happened so fast. There was a blur, and they shoved me against the wall, and then you were on them." I shuddered. I didn't want to keep thinking about it. A part of me hoped it was some misunderstanding, some completely unrelated crime, and it was just a horrible coincidence that I feared assassins in the dark. Then my mind caught up to what Zyrus was saying. "*You* checked the system? How? You're not in station security."

He flexed his hand, flashing his fingers. "I have certain skills. I didn't always live on Nebula Outpost."

He'd been a soldier once.

Had he told me that? Someone must have. I tried to chase the thought down, but it disappeared into the morass that was my mind.

"So, you just hacked into a secure system like it was nothing?"

"The station's system is hardly secure. They ignore basic updates and run most of their data off of cheap equipment that is better suited to manage orders in a restaurant. I'm certain I'm not the only person with access who shouldn't have it." He sipped his drink.

Well, that wasn't comforting.

It was midday, and I'd already napped once. We had no leads on who'd attacked me the day before, and I had a feeling Zyrus would be happy to stay in my quarters for the rest of the day and do nothing. It was easiest to keep me safe that way. But if we did that, I'd go stir crazy.

I'd gotten used to walking the perimeter of our encampment, multiple miles over steep terrain every day. Of course, being cooped up on a space station was driving me a little crazy.

"Have you heard anything about the others down on Nebula?" They should have been up here by now. It had been *weeks*.

"I'm afraid not."

Then that gave me a place to start. I stood. "Let's go, then."

Zyrus didn't argue, but he did ask, "Go where?"

"I'm going to annoy station security until they tell me why my friends aren't here yet." If nothing else, at least poking that nest of hornets would be something to do.

"Are you certain that's a good idea?" He didn't try to stop me as I headed for the door, but he slipped out in front to scout the hallway for threats.

"They've been stranded down there for a decade; they shouldn't have to wait any longer." I chose a direction and marched off, realizing a few steps in that I wasn't exactly sure where the main station security offices were. But Zyrus pointed me in the right direction, and we were there in only a few minutes.

Of course, the head of security was busy. As was his second. And anyone else who might be able to shed some light on the situation.

I crossed my eyes and glared at the schedule board outside the office.

"We can schedule an appointment," Zyrus suggested.

But at that same moment, the door to the main security offices opened, and two security officers stepped out. They barely glanced at Zyrus and me.

I moved before I truly thought through the action, catching the door before it could close and walking through. Zyrus made a sound in the back of his throat, as if he was about to yell at me to stop but thought better of it.

The offices were a bit barren, and few people were sitting at desks. We passed what must have been a break room where several security officers were sitting around a table and playing some sort of game that involved holograms. No one tried to stop us.

The schedule board had listed the number of the head of security's office, and I was headed straight to it.

"This isn't wise," Zyrus warned before I put my hand over the sensor to open the door.

I ignored him.

The door opened, which was surprising in and of itself. Even more surprising, a man sat with his feet propped on the desk, his chair tipped back and head lolling. He jerked when he heard us enter the room.

Commander Henner.

We'd met when his men had interrogated me after my rescue, as if I was some sort of threat to the station. He hadn't made a good impression then, and somehow, I wasn't shocked to find him sleeping on the job.

"What are you doing in here?" he barked. He dropped his feet to the floor and stood, his chair slamming back into the wall. "Who are you? What do you want?" His glare might have dissuaded someone else, but I'd been through enough that it didn't bother me.

I took the seat opposite his. Zyrus remained standing behind me, my sentinel. "Don't you remember me, Commander Henner?"

The glare lessened a smidge, but he remained standing, as if looking down at me might make me feel small. "There are thousands of people on this station, ma'am. You don't want me remembering you."

"There are a hundred people down on Nebula that you promised to bring back. I'm here to see why my friends are still stuck down there." I didn't raise my voice, but it was a close thing.

Recognition bloomed. "You're that woman. Right. I'm glad to see you've healed up nicely." He took his seat once more and pulled up his tablet. "I understand you've been through a lot. This isn't how things are done on Nebula, but I can do this as a favor ... for all you've suffered." He glanced up at Zyrus, cleared his throat, and then back down at his tablet.

I was tempted to look at the Detyen behind me. What was his face doing to make Henner so agreeable?

"Thank you," I said. "Sir," I added for good measure. Henner was clearly a lazy man, but his uniform was well pressed, and he had a framed commendation from Nebula Enterprises on his wall. He cared about his rank.

And his shoulders pulled back a little at the respect, posture straightening.

"Ah, here it is," he said after a few moments of scrolling. "Yes, we have the record of your report, and security is liaising with the health team to institute the proper quarantine procedures. We need to ensure no one brings a communicable disease to the ship. I hope you understand. Merely a precaution."

"A quarantine? No one's sick." I knew the health of my people very well.

"A precaution," he repeated. "Once they've been cleared, we can make space for them here, get them in in contact with their families. It just takes time."

"How much time?" My friends were a twenty-minute transport ship ride away, and yet it felt like light years.

"That will be determined by medical. Shall I put a note in the file to update you when transport begins?" His hand hovered over his tablet.

"Yes. Can I at least talk to someone down there? Let them know I'm alright?"

"The equipment is limited. We can't have anyone making social calls. I'll make certain you're updated when things begin to move forward. Will that be all?" He raised an eyebrow. No matter how this meeting had started, the commander felt in control now.

I wanted to scream, to demand he produce my friends this instant. But I'd already gotten lucky once by barging into his office. There was no reason to test my luck again. "Thank you." He didn't deserve a second *sir*.

Zyrus and I left, the commander's words echoing in my head.

"You're troubled," Zyrus observed as we left the security hub and headed back towards my quarters.

"What he said was bullshit." Every step I took made it more clear to me. "We spent a decade down on that planet, and no one got so much as a cold or a flu. How could we? There were no vectors of infection, nothing to make us sick. If anyone *did* get sick, it was from their own bodies: kidney stones, cancer, a seizure. Horrible, but nothing that could harm anyone else. And medical wasn't concerned with me or Alice passing anything on. If my people are quarantined, it's not for illness."

"Then what for?"

"I wish I knew."

5
ZYRUS

I DIDN'T KNOW where to go. Pippa had arrived at Astrid's quarters a few moments ago and unceremoniously kicked me out, stating she and Astrid were due for some "girl time." Astrid had shot me a look I had trouble reading, but she hadn't asked me to stay. So, I left.

And now I was sitting quietly on a bench in the hallway, unsure of my next move.

I should feel the bond by now. The recognition had been all consuming eleven years ago. All that had existed for me was Astrid. And now she looked like just any other woman.

What if I was wrong? What if she wasn't my mate? Certainly, she looked like the woman I'd met on Honora Station all those years ago, but it was a big galaxy. She might merely be a stranger wearing my mate's face.

No, that wasn't right. Astrid was no stranger to me, even if I couldn't feel the bond between us. And to say she was just like any other woman belied the situation.

There were no other women.

Not to me.

I didn't see anyone like that, knowing I should want them, knowing my body belonged to them, knowing they owned my soul if I still had it.

No one but Astrid. Not since the moment I'd seen her eleven years ago.

I'd been a typical warrior before that—cocky, headstrong, and eager for all the attention that came with the position. After I recognized her as my mate, though, I hadn't wanted anyone but her.

So why didn't I feel the recognition? We'd been near each other for over a week now. I'd spent nearly every waking hour with her. It should have been there. Instead, all I had to show for it was pain when we touched and a bloody nose.

I needed advice. If there was one person on the station who could shed light on this situation, it was

Drex. He'd proven the impossible possible when he found his mate in Pippa. Even I had been skeptical. Yes, I'd known my mate was out there, but I'd recognized her before I sacrificed my soul. It had never occurred to me that someone might find their denya when all was lost.

Still, I hesitated. In the Legion, any deviation from expected conduct could mean the end of a soulless warrior. Each of the men on this station had received a death sentence already, and we were the lucky ones, each smuggled out by someone who recognized the injustice in our situation. Old habits died hard. I hadn't spoken a word of Astrid to anyone after the procedure, and still looking for her had earned me my death sentence.

Speaking to Drex seemed like a risk, even if he was the last person on the ship likely to do me harm. And if anyone would understand, it would be him.

I stood and went to his and Pippa's door, hesitating for only another moment before I knocked.

He answered. "Pippa said she was visiting Astrid. Did she kick you out?" His lips tugged into a small smile, something that was still strange to see on his face.

"Yes." With Astrid, I was becoming comfortable

with elaborating, but it was something the soulless rarely did.

"Would you like to sit in here while they talk?" He gestured to the couch.

"That's not why I came." Though, perhaps it was a good idea. It could disturb people to see me sitting outside Astrid's door like some kind of guard dog. I entered the apartment and took a seat.

Drex sat in the chair beside the couch and waited. He may have regained his emotions, but he could be as silent and patient as the soulless when necessary.

I didn't know how to start. A decade ago, I had kept my mouth shut about meeting Astrid in some pique of hurt pride, my ego wounded in the way that only a twenty-three-year-old man's ego can be. I'd been hurt and angry, and a little ashamed. I'd had my denya in my grasp, and she'd disappeared in a puff of smoke. Not to mention, I'd never heard of a Detyen finding a human denya, not back then. It had all seemed a bit like a dream.

Speaking the truth now when I couldn't feel it seemed like a lie.

"Is something troubling you?" Drex finally asked. I must have been quiet for some time.

"Your bond with Pippa, how did that happen?

When did you recognize her?" I hadn't paid much attention at the time. Though Drex had asked me to lend my skills with computer systems, I hadn't been involved in his personal life.

His eyebrows shot up and he gave me a closer look. "That's an interesting question. Do you think—"

"Astrid is my mate." We could sit here all day dancing around the subject, so perhaps it was best to put everything in the open. "We briefly met while I was on leave eleven years ago. I recognized her then. She disappeared before we could seal the bond between us, or even have a discussion about it. I spent the rest of my time in the Legion looking for her, and I never found her because she was stranded on a planet and cut off from all communication. I know who she is to me, but I don't ... feel it." The last two words were barely more than a whisper. I was soulless. I'd been outcast from the Legion for acting out.

Admitting that I expected to feel something was asking for death.

But I wasn't in the Legion anymore. And Drex was the last person on this station who would kill me.

He was silent for several moments, hands

steepled together as he considered what I'd told him. "That is ..."

"Don't say impossible."

"I wasn't going to. I hardly could, given my own situation. There is no path for this. I can only tell you what happened to me. Ryklin may have more to say on the matter. We have not compared notes." He blew out a breath. "What is your emotional state so far? Have you felt anything out of the ordinary?"

I couldn't answer it, and this time it had nothing to do with old Legion prohibitions. What was the difference between feeling and wanting to feel? From wanting and wanting to want?

"It hurts when I touch her." I could give him the facts. "I almost kissed her the other day, and my nose started to bleed. When she has a nightmare, I run into the room like there's an enemy I can fight. I hesitated before leaving her alone with Pippa. Is that what you're asking?" My own actions laid bare sounded like nothing.

"I felt that pain," said Drex. "The first time I kissed Pippa, I passed out. I've wondered if that was caused by something in my brain coming back to life, some sort of pathway being created by the bond. This will be the last thing you wish to hear, but I think you need to be patient, to let this run its course. When you've healed enough to truly bond with her, you'll know."

"You truly think we need to heal? That whatever was done to us could be undone by the denya bond?"

"I'm living proof. So is Ryklin. I'm sorry I can't give you more answers."

"If I'm healing, do you think that could undo whatever circumvented the Denya Price? Could I drop dead if I don't claim Astrid?" The Denya Price was the thing that haunted every Detyen. If we reached thirty without finding our mates, we died. Or those of us in the Legion could choose to become soulless.

"I don't know. But you can't force whatever is happening. Stay close to Astrid. Let your instincts guide you."

"I'm soulless, I don't have instincts."

He huffed out a laugh. "We both know that's a lie."

There wasn't much more to say after that. Pippa was supposed to return to her quarters once she was done with Astrid, but more than an hour went by, and she didn't come back. I could have used the time to do anything else except stew in my confusion, but I remained in Drex's quarters, thinking.

Thinking too much would drive me mad.

I left, those instincts that no soulless was supposed to have driving me down the hall just as Pippa and Astrid slipped out of Astrid's room and started heading in the opposite direction. Neither had said anything about leaving the room, and someone was still after Astrid.

But I didn't call after them. Pippa knew this ship better than just about anyone, and she'd survived the horrors it could throw at her. Astrid was relatively safe with her.

That didn't mean I let them go alone. But I hung back, nearly out of sight, and let them wander. As the hallways around us grew more crowded, I suspected they were heading towards one of the entertainment hubs.

We'd walked for several minutes when I realized someone was following them. The stranger was half a hallway in front of me, wearing a maintenance uniform and carrying a broom. But they walked around three different pieces of refuse that had been haphazardly kicked aside, and when Astrid and Pippa paused to read an announcement board on the wall, the alleged maintenance person paused with them and began to sweep.

Surveillance. And not too subtle.

When Pippa and Astrid walked on, so too did their follower. And when they paused again, so did the alleged maintenance tech.

I was a trained former member of the Detyen Legion. I could follow a target without being obvious. But whoever this was, they were sloppy and unprofessional.

I didn't want someone tracking my mate's every move. It was my responsibility to keep her safe, but I hesitated. This follower was only watching, not attacking. And we needed information about whoever wanted to harm Astrid.

This was my chance.

I got a little closer and waited for my moment.

Then the maintenance tech abandoned their broom and ducked into a restroom. Astrid and Pippa weren't paying any attention; they hadn't noticed their stalker.

Stalkers, technically.

It was a single occupancy restroom, so I couldn't barge in and ask my questions. Instead, I waited just in sight of the door. And a few minutes later, a woman walked out wearing a station security uniform and carrying a bag over her shoulder.

She walked by the way she came, not sparing a glance at Astrid or Pippa, and opened a door labeled RESTRICTED before I could make a move to stop her.

Why was someone in station security watching my mate?

6

ASTRID

PIPPA TRIED to argue when I said I needed to do this alone. Maybe it was foolish, but I hadn't had time alone, really alone, since I'd gotten here. I knew everyone was trying to help me. And being with Zyrus in my quarters wasn't nearly as grating as I might have expected.

But I'd spent ten years with easy access to privacy. Too much privacy sometimes, but solitude had a way of growing on a person.

I wasn't going anywhere dangerous or out of the way. If someone tried to attack me, I'd be in screaming distance of a crowd. It was both a refreshing and terrifying thought.

I couldn't stop trying to puzzle out what Commander Henner meant about the quarantine down on Nebula. And it had occurred to me that the best people to give me answers worked in the medical wing.

The place was bustling with activity as I approached.

What I was about to do wasn't exactly the most ethical, but I couldn't think of another way to talk to someone that day.

I went to the check-in desk and signed in, requesting to talk to the doctor who'd treated me weeks ago with a complaint about pain where I'd been shot. There was only a robot sitting at reception, so I couldn't appeal to anyone's sympathy. Instead, I had to sit and wait.

But my name must have been flagged in the system, or it was a slow day. Dr. Morel called me back after only a few moments, and I was seated on an exam table with my shirt hiked up before I could say I was fine.

"There's a bit of redness, but that's to be expected," she told me, her hands firm and cool. "I don't see anything externally that worries me, but we should do a scan to see if something has gone wrong inside." She stood.

I reached out and touched her arm. "Please, Doctor. I actually had a couple questions."

"I should put the order in first, then I'll be right back." She looked down at my hand like it offended her.

I didn't let go. "I'm not actually experiencing any pain. I needed to talk to you about the quarantine down on Nebula."

Her face went blank. She looked over her shoulder as if to confirm the door was closed, that we weren't being listened to. "What are you talking about? I'm a busy woman."

"I asked Commander Henner why no one from Nebula has come up to the station yet. He said there was some kind of quarantine. But we haven't been exposed to anything. Believe me, I'd know if sickness ran through my encampment. Anything serious could have wiped us out. I thought you could give me an idea of what they think the problem is and when the quarantine might be lifted." I dropped my hand. Tears threatened to prick at my eyes, but I wouldn't let them. I felt desperate and angry and small, and I hated it.

Dr. Morel's face softened. "I'm not involved in any quarantine down on Nebula, nor are any of my staff. I inquired about those down on Nebula shortly after you were released from my care, and I was told it was handled and to not speak of it again.

If they're being quarantined, it isn't for medical reasons."

Damn it.

I believed the doctor far more than I believed Commander Henner. And it confirmed my suspicions. Something was wrong on the planet, and my people were in danger.

But what could I do about it?

I left the medical wing and started walking back to my quarters. Only a few moments later, I passed by two station security members who each gave me a friendly nod. I didn't return it. I wasn't feeling too friendly.

I needed to find out what was going on down on Nebula. Or at least I needed to find a way to communicate, or to get them supplies. Our comms had been jammed for years by the people running an illegal mining operation out of the defunct mine. There shouldn't be jammers anymore. All they needed was the equipment.

Were they down there alone? Or was station security down there guarding them like they'd done something wrong?

We were victims of a disaster; we didn't deserve this.

The skin on the back of my neck prickled in

awareness as I realized I was being followed. I spun around, ready for ... something. Or not. But there stood Zyrus, an almost angry look on his normally blank face.

"You were supposed to stay with Pippa," he said. The words came out harsher than I'd ever heard him speak.

"I had to run an errand." He was guarding me, but I wasn't going to let him become my jailer. "I needed some time alone."

"Then you can ask me to leave the room." He turned his head slightly, pausing to listen to something, then charged forward and crowded me close. We were in a small alcove, almost hidden from the rest of the hallway. "There are people after you, Astrid. You can't be walking alone."

"I am a grown woman. And I was in public the whole time. Do you really think someone is going to murder me in a crowd?"

"They could. Sometimes it's easier that way. One person gets close, hits you with a modified blaster shot or some kind of poison. Then you're down before anyone knows what happened." His eyes flashed red, lips pulled back in a scowl. "I am here to protect you."

We were close. Too close for this fight. I could

smell the masculine scent of him, something strangely woodsy even though we were on this station miles above the trees. My heart raced in my chest, and I realized he wasn't angry. He was scared.

For me.

I swallowed. "Okay."

"Okay what?"

"You can protect me. I fucked up. I shouldn't have gone alone."

His shoulders relaxed a fraction, but he didn't back down.

The tension morphed from anger and fear to something hotter, something full of possibility. I was still staring at him, memorizing the planes of his face. But that face wasn't new. It felt like there was a space missing in my mind, a Zyrus shaped hole that had somehow been covered up for all these years and was only now found again.

How could it feel like I'd missed him when we didn't know one another? How could it feel like he'd been holding a piece of me I hadn't known I'd lost?

I reached up and traced my fingers over his cheek. The heat of his skin seared me, and for a moment, I thought I could feel something, a spark.

Zyrus's eyes were still red, and he was breathing deep. He leaned in, and I thought he'd kiss me, but instead he buried his face in the crook of my neck, nuzzling me.

I clutched his shoulder. We couldn't do this here. Anyone could see us.

But he didn't seem to notice, didn't seem to care.

He inhaled deeply, like he was trying to memorize my scent. His lips brushed my neck, and I shivered.

Then he yanked himself back with a pained sound in the back of his throat. He turned away from me and back towards the hallway. Then his entire body stiffened.

Then he took off running, chasing something I couldn't see.

7

ZYRUS

INSTINCT HAD me running before I could fully comprehend the situation. But I recognized the woman in that uniform. She was the same person who'd been stalking Astrid earlier. This couldn't be a coincidence.

I had to trust that Astrid would stay put. After expressing my displeasure at her going off alone, I knew I was a hypocrite to leave her.

Too late now.

I turned a corner just in time to see the woman dart down a hallway. I was attracting attention, but I didn't care. I needed answers.

The woman ducked into a service corridor, the kind that was off-limits to regular station personnel.

It was narrow, and I slammed into the wall as I took the corner too fast. I couldn't see her anymore.

That didn't stop me. I could still catch up.

But I passed several doors that could have lead anywhere before I hit a dead end.

No woman. No answers.

Damn it.

I had to force myself to stop and take several deep breaths as something inside me roiled. My head felt ready to explode with ... something. Frustration? Anger? Any emotion? It *hurt*, like a limb coming back after falling asleep. Pins and needles and pain.

I reveled in it, in any sign that the thing between Astrid and myself was real.

Astrid.

No more time to wallow. I sprinted back, retracing my path to the small alcove I'd been in only minutes before. But she was gone.

That static in my head reared up again, and I looked around, jerking to and fro for some hint of her. Had this been some ploy to distract me to grab her? I should have never left her alone.

I had to do something, comb the floor for any hint of what might have happened.

But I made myself pause. This area was busy,

and no one seemed to think anything strange had happened. Then again, if station security had apprehended a person, who would care?

There was an Oscavian sitting on a bench outside of the medical wing. I approached them cautiously. "Excuse me, did you see where the woman I was speaking with went?"

The Oscavian looked up at me with her bright blue eyes set in deep purple skin. Her face carried the wrinkles of age, and her hair was mostly a dark violet but was lavender around her skull. "That girl you ran away from? She looked pissed. She walked away a few minutes ago. Headed that way." She pointed down the main hallway.

"Alone?"

The Oscavian nodded.

"Thank you."

That didn't calm the miasma of feeling inside of me. Astrid could still be in danger. But she'd walked away alone, which meant she probably wasn't in immediate danger.

But she'd walked away *right* after we'd discussed why she shouldn't.

Frustrating woman.

I headed towards her quarters. If she was going anywhere, it would be there. And that was confirmed when I made it to her hallway just in time to see her putting in the security code to open her door.

She saw me, and her eyes widened, but she didn't try to slam the door.

Something pounded in my temples, and my fists were clenched. My jaw was tight, right along with the rest of my body. I was primed for a fight. But this was my mate. I'd never lay a finger on her. So, what was my body doing? I tried to relax, tried to breathe deeply and let all the tension out.

Any progress I made was washed away the moment I remembered that empty alcove.

"You said you wouldn't go anywhere alone." My tone was even. Normal. I ignored the fact that my jaw was so tight it hurt.

Astrid scowled. "Nice lecture. Maybe don't leave me alone the second you give it. What the hell was that?" She crossed her arms, chin raised. She was angry, defiant.

"Someone was following you. I saw them earlier today and then just now. The woman works in station security." Facts, that was what I needed. Astrid would understand.

But something about what I said made her mouth drop open. "Earlier today? Were you following Pippa and me? You said you'd leave us alone."

"I happened to leave Drex's room at the same time you were both walking down the hallway. It's my job to protect you, Astrid. Did I try to stop you?" I wanted to reach out and clutch her close, to make her understand the severity of today.

"I don't want you stalking me." She glared and then turned away from me.

"I wasn't stalking you, but some woman from station security was. And if you want to get rid of me, you need to let me do my job. The sooner we get to the bottom of this, the sooner I'll be gone."

She turned back at that, her breathing a bit ragged and eyes wide. "I don't—" She cut herself off. "That's not what we're talking about. You're not going anywhere."

I stepped forward and placed a gentle hand on her arm. "I just want to protect you. We both know that something strange is going on. Once we figure that out ..." I didn't know how to finish the sentence. I wasn't walking away from her once this job was done. She was my mate—the woman I'd been searching out for eleven years. I would lay down my life for hers, anything she wanted.

But I didn't say the words.

She still didn't recognize me.

Astrid raised her hand to my cheek, the action identical to what she'd done just a little while ago in the alcove. It burned like her hand was covered in hot coals, and I leaned into the pain. "What makes me so special?" she asked. "I don't think you're like this with anyone else."

She had no idea.

I could tell her. Three words. *You're my mate.* It explained everything. But those words caught in my throat. It took me a moment to realize why.

I was a selfish bastard.

I would have said the soulless couldn't be selfish, but we were still people, no matter how our brains were broken.

Ever since I'd set eyes on Astrid, I'd been focused on the mating bond that I couldn't feel, focused on that memory that had lived in my mind for eleven years. I'd been obsessed with making her mine, claiming her, convinced it would happen so long as I stayed beside her. And guarding her provided the perfect opportunity.

As if love was bound to bloom in forced proximity.

But Astrid was human. A human woman who had been stranded on a planet with no hope of escape for a decade. A human woman who was worried that someone was hunting her for unknown reasons. A human woman who couldn't feel the recognition of the denya bond.

Of course she didn't remember that day on Honora Station. And I needed to leave it in the past.

I didn't have words for her. Instead, I pulled her close, enveloping her in my embrace.

I would keep this woman safe. And I would find a way to be worthy of her, to make her want me in the present instead of clinging to the past.

My body lit up with pain everywhere we touched, but Astrid relaxed against me, and it was all worth it.

8
ASTRID

I'D BEEN HERE BEFORE.

This place looked nothing like Nebula Outpost. People were bustling like they had some place to be, and the number of shops and restaurants dwarfed the options I was getting used to.

"Flight 05-93-402-A to the Nebula Mining Colony is delayed. Updates will be sent to your communication device and will be posted on boards across the station. We appreciate your understanding." The voice on the intercom was a blast from the past.

I was on Honora Station on my trip to Nebula. How could I forget?

It was a hazy mix of dream and memory, this day blotted out by the tragedy that would happen only a few months later. But it had been a good one. I remembered that.

I started moving without thinking about it, heading away from the gate, following the flow of bodies to the main part of the station. There was somewhere I had to be. Someone I had to see.

But that was strange. I didn't know anyone on Honora Station. This was just another stopover in a life of stopovers.

I felt a tug on my chest and glanced down, but there was nothing there, the sensation a phantom conjured up by my mind. Still, I followed it. What else was I supposed to do?

And there he was.

Oh.

Right.

He was taller than me, and teal, with dark spots covering his arms like some strange tattoo or animal's spots. His dark hair was cut short, and he carried himself like he was the king of the world.

Then he looked at me and smiled.

My heart rate kicked up as something like recognition lit me up from inside. I could have sworn I knew this guy, but I'd never seen anyone like him.

He sauntered up to me, the confidence slipping

to something almost like wonder. Just from looking at me.

If I didn't say something, I was going to do something crazy with my mouth. And I couldn't just launch myself at this stranger and start kissing him, could I? What was going on? Since when did I have this *need*?

"Good evening," I said, searching for anything and landing on the most asinine. "Or morning? What time is it? I'm sorry. I've been traveling for a week." I hadn't paid attention to the clocks, and each space station had a different time zone. It was hard to keep track when you were bouncing from place to place too fast for your sleep cycle to catch up.

"What time do you want it to be?" He was still looking at me with that open wonder, and his hand twitched as if he might reach out and touch me.

I wanted that.

I swallowed hard. "Are you the welcoming committee? Because this is stranger than any port I've landed at so far." Did that sound like an insult? What was I even trying to say? "Good, though. I think. Do I know you?" There was this nagging sensation in the back of my mind that I *had* to. Of course I knew ... this guy. I'd just been waiting to meet him.

"You will." He held out his hand. "Let me show you around the place."

My flight could be rescheduled for any moment, and if I missed it, I'd be out an incredibly lucrative job. "I have to ..." But I didn't want to miss out on whatever this was. "I don't even know your name."

"I'm Zyrus. I can call my friend Kyric if you need a reference." His eyebrows drooped for a second, a funny look on his face, but it cleared. "What's your name?"

"Astrid."

I went with him.

I knew this was real, and I knew it was a dream. Half memory, half something else entirely.

And that's when it started to get hazy around the edges. Because Zyrus didn't lead me up to a rented room. He didn't smile and quirk that eyebrow when we kissed.

But we took the lift up to the penthouse, as if space stations *had* penthouses, our hands linked.

Then we were in a room mostly made up of a bed, and all I could focus on was him. He wrapped his arms around me, lips trailing over my neck as he spoke. "I've waited forever for you."

I wanted to say it back, but I didn't know why. In the dream, I'd only known him for moments. This wasn't real.

But my body was heavy with need. Heat pooled in my core, and Zyrus's hands wandered over my skin like he couldn't touch enough of me.

My clothes melted away, and Zyrus's hands were on me, teasing, caressing. I stopped worrying about what was real or not. All I knew was pleasure.

He pushed me back on the bed and crawled up my body, lips meeting mine in a kiss that was fire and lightning all rolled into one. His tongue traced my bottom lip, and I arched up, wanting more.

Zyrus trailed kisses down my neck, his lips hot and perfect. I tangled my hands in his hair and held him to me, needing him. I was on fire with need, every sensation piling up until it was hard to think about anything but him.

His lips trailed lower, sucking at my nipple until I cried out, pleasure racing through me.

"Zyrus." I needed him, all of him. Now.

But he took his time, kissing down my belly and spreading my legs. His tongue flicked over my sex, and I arched up, crying out.

How could he know how to perfectly touch me

like this? How could this moment be everything I needed?

It didn't matter.

He teased me, licking and sucking until I was nearly insane with need. I could go insane with this kind of want.

Then his fingers replaced his tongue, and the strokes filled me up, spreading me wide as I whimpered and clutched at him.

"Please," I begged. I needed him.

"Soon, denya."

That word. It meant something. I'd heard it before, I knew that. I must have. It echoed around in my mind, and I should ask him. But I was strung tight, ready to snap, and it would only take one more brush of his hand for me to explode with pleasure.

Then Zyrus was over me, his cock teasing my entrance as he looked down at me with eyes that glowed red.

A loudspeaker broke through the fantasy. "Flight 05-93-402-A to the Nebula Mining Colony is preparing to leave. Passengers must report to Gate 137 immediately to ensure that we do not lose our departure window."

In a blink and without a thought, I was dressed again, suddenly in the middle of a hallway and fleeing something I couldn't comprehend. And then I was seated on a ship, buckled in and headed for my future.

Leaving my destiny behind.

My eyes snapped open, and I was disoriented for only a moment, but this was real. Nebula Outpost.

Zyrus.

He wasn't in the room. Already, the dream was starting to slip away, but I grabbed hold tight and reached for my comm, trying to write down anything I remembered.

We'd met that day on Honora Station. We'd kissed.

How could I forget?

Eleven years was a long time, especially when so many of them had been dedicated to eking out a survival on a planet completely indifferent to me and my people.

But there was something important to that meeting with Zyrus, something that had left its mark on both of us. What had changed him from that smiling, flirtatious young man to the serious, cold ex-soldier he was today? Who had hurt him?

If I wanted to know, I'd need to figure out what it all meant. I just didn't know if I was ready to face it.

9
ASTRID

I COULDN'T STOP LOOKING at Zyrus, and I wanted to blame the dream. That dream haunted me, and like all true hauntings, it had a nasty habit of sneaking up on me and then dissolving into nothing when I tried to examine it too closely.

If Zyrus noticed anything different in the following days, he didn't say a word. He was just there, my silent shadow.

It should have been annoying.

It wasn't.

I wanted to touch him. When he sat on my sofa and merely existed, it took all of my willpower to keep my hands to myself. It was even worse when he stood. It seemed like every day, we'd somehow end up only a foot apart, staring into each other's eyes and waiting for something to happen.

He was looking at me too. Never at the same time. I looked at him, but I could feel his eyes on me as I tried to keep myself busy. That was the other thing. I was starting to go stir crazy. It had been weeks since my injury, and I was plenty healed. I was used to walking the perimeter of the encampment every day on guard duty or just to stretch my legs. There was always something that needed to be done down on Nebula, some fire to put out—figuratively or literally.

I needed a job or something like it, somewhere to keep me occupied so I couldn't worry about what was happening on Nebula or keep obsessing over the blue giant who had taken up residence in my quarters and my mind. But that felt like a big step, like I was admitting I planned to stay on Nebula Outpost for some time.

If there was danger here, I knew I shouldn't stay. But this was where Zyrus was, and something felt undeniably wrong about walking away from him without giving it—whatever it was—a chance.

"Is everything alright?" Zyrus asked. He was sitting on the sofa with a tablet in his hand. The screen was lit with bright colors and cartoons.

"Are you playing a game?" He normally sat quietly or peered at the viewscreen on the wall as if it showed the actual outside instead of a projected image.

"It tests my reflexes. It keeps my mind sharp."

"But is it fun?" It had been years since I had a tablet or comm with enough charge to play one of the ubiquitous games out there, but I'd had favorites for the long days of travel between jobs back in the day.

He turned off the screen and set the tablet down to look at me fully, his brows drawn down a bit as if that question was confusing. "It is intellectual stimulation."

He was nothing like the man I'd met on Honora Station.

The thought walloped me on the side, and I nearly staggered as if it was something physical. Was that dream real? Some sort of mixed up memory? I'd traveled across the galaxy more than once, and every place tended to blend into every other place. Coming off a days-long journey in cheap accommodations and landing at yet another space station wasn't worth remembering.

But Zyrus was. How could I have forgotten?

But it still didn't feel real enough for me to say

something. And if we'd met before and Zyrus remembered, surely he would have said something by now. Maybe I'd met someone who looked like him, another Detyen who'd tried to turn my head.

It didn't feel right.

I wished the dream was a bit easier to remember, or that there wasn't a decade of trauma piled on top of it making excavation of the memory nearly impossible.

"Do you ever just do something for fun?" He was so serious all the time. I knew he was there to guard me, but no one was going to break down my door, and if that was something Zyrus was even remotely concerned about, he wouldn't have been playing a game.

"Fun is not ... " He trailed off with a shake of his head, as if he didn't know how to finish the sentence.

"You haven't always been this way." I should have made it a question, but it came out as a statement. "How'd you get so serious?"

He was quiet for several moments, and I thought he wouldn't answer. Finally, he did. "It was the only way I could survive."

There was pain in that statement, and I wanted to delve into it, to uncover all of Zyrus's secrets, but I forced myself not to ask. We all had our pain, and it was never any fun when someone went poking around in it.

"I said I'd check in on Alice today. Do you mind if we ...?" I nodded towards the door. The room felt heavy with unsaid things, and it was best if we left for a bit. Who knew what I would say if I didn't walk out.

Zyrus stood and left his tablet on the side table. We walked in silence to Alice's room, and I knocked.

"I'll wait over there for you." He pointed towards a bench. "Please don't leave without me."

"Right. Sure." No more solo jaunts. I'd agreed to that.

Zyrus walked towards the bench, and Alice answered the door. She gave a questioning look to his fleeing back but didn't say anything. Her quarters were only a hallway over from mine, but they were about half the size, and she didn't even have a private space for her bedroom. The place was tidy, both because neither Alice nor I had many things to mess a place up and because she'd always been fastidious.

"Any luck—"

"Have you—"

We both spoke at the same time, cutting each other off. I shut my mouth and let her speak.

"Have you contacted anyone down on Nebula?" she asked. She took a seat on one of the two chairs in her small dining area, and I took the other one.

"Not yet. Something weird is going on." I told her all I'd learned so far, the alleged quarantine, and what the doctor said. It wasn't much, but what I knew wasn't good either.

"I knew that job was too good to be true." She scowled it out.

That had become something of a mantra down on Nebula. The pay at the Nebula mine had been good, good enough to attract people from across the galaxy into leaving their lives behind for difficult, dangerous work. For a while, some people had even thought the explosion was some sort of inside job to keep from paying us. I could never quite believe that, but with the way things were going now, maybe the conspiracy theorists had a point.

"I'm trying to find out more," I promised. "It's just hard from up here."

"Harder down there."

"Yeah." We had easy access to food and water, to soap and bathtubs and everything I'd wanted for ten years of hard living. Complaining while we were stuck up here was not a good look. "Any luck contacting your family?" Unlike me, Alice had left behind people who cared about her to take a one-year contract at the mine.

"I've found a new address. They moved. It appears my wife remarried."

"Oh, Alice. I'm sorry to hear that." I reached out and covered her hand with mine, offering a squeeze.

Strangely, she smiled. "Namyra was a good friend of ours, a *very* good friend, if you know what I mean. We'll have to see how things go when I get back, whether there's something to pull out of the ashes."

A wife back home and a lover, from the sounds of it. At least Alice would be taken care of.

"What's going on with you and the big blue guy?" Alice asked. She picked up a piece of paper on her side table and folded it and refolded it until it was limp in her hands.

"You know what's going on, you were there." Alice had come right along when I was injured, not leaving my side until I was rushed into surgery. She'd been one of the first to know that Zyrus agreed to watch me.

"It's been weeks. I understand your concerns, but don't you think we're too, I don't know, insignificant, for someone to hunt down? Once news of Nebula gets out, there will be a few media stories, maybe a few lawsuits, and that's it. It will disappear under a thousand other stories, and no one will remember it by next year. They've probably all forgotten about the disaster."

I wished I had an answer to that. Maybe I was being paranoid, but now that I had memories of Zyrus lurking in the back of my mind, I didn't want to send him away. Not until I figured this out.

I could tell Alice.

It was on the tip of my tongue. Yes, Noelle and Pippa both had Detyen lovers and knew what it was like to be in a relationship, but Alice knew *me*. We'd spent a decade together eking out survival on a planet completely indifferent to us, and that bound people together in a way beyond friendship. She'd listen to me.

Or she'd just tell me to fuck the man and see how things went. We weren't trapped any more.

"I'm going to keep trying to find a way to get word to the others," I said. I couldn't talk about Zyrus; I didn't know how to put it into words.

But with that done, there was nothing more to say.

Zyrus was waiting for me just as he'd promised

and stood from the bench when I slid out of the room. He turned toward my quarters, but I shook my head.

"I need to walk, need to clear my thoughts, just for a bit." I wasn't asking. If he told me no, I might scream.

He nodded and kept pace beside me silently.

I couldn't keep my mouth shut. "If I don't keep pushing station security, no one is getting off of Nebula. It's too easy to forget about them down there. I'm tempted to hijack a ship and go and rescue them myself." I paused and blew out a breath. "But my flying skills aren't exactly great. Can you pilot?"

"Yes." The word was completely neutral, with no hint on whether he wanted to help or stop me.

"What do you think they'd do if I showed up with a hundred refugees and told them to deal with it?" There was an image in my head of blazing blasters and red-faced captains. It would be satisfying until they threw me onto a penal colony and made me disappear forever.

"It's more than a hundred, isn't it?" he reminded me. "With the prisoners who were kept in the mine."

Did it make me a bad person that I forgot about them? I didn't ask the question out loud because I feared I knew the answer. "Right."

But the extra survivors down on the planet just made this whole thing worse. Why weren't they being brought to Nebula Outpost so they could be sent home?

Zyrus placed his hand on my sleeve, and I looked up at him. His face was as serious as always, but looking at him made my breath catch in my throat.

He was gorgeous.

Had I really kissed that mouth all those years ago or was that just the dream?

He nodded towards a door I hadn't noticed and tugged on my sleeve just enough to get me to take a step that way. I felt its absence when his hand dropped away.

I wasn't sure what I was expecting when the door slid open, but it wasn't a comms closet. One whole wall was made up of screens and buttons, but no one was there to stop us from touching anything.

"What is this place?" Nebula Outpost seemed to have been built with hidden away rooms in mind.

"The rooms weren't originally wired for long-distance comms," he explained as he touched the screen to make it light up. "These closets used to be available for rent for people who wanted to call back to planets outside the Nebula system. Most of the closets have been repurposed, but for some reason they've kept a few." He adjusted a dial, and the screen came to life, though it was only showing the logo of the space station.

"Are you ... What are you doing?" For some reason, my mind couldn't keep up, and all I could do was watch Zyrus's hands as they worked.

"I'm trying to contact one of the comm stations down on Nebula. Ryklin was able to message from an outpost, and I know those coordinates, but there's no guarantee that the equipment survived the fight or that anyone's manning the station."

"You're getting me in touch with my people?"

"I'm trying."

My eyes widened, and my heart started to pound. There was space for a chair in front of the screen, but if there ever had been one in this closet, it had been moved a long time ago.

At first, I heard static, but after a moment, it resolved into a man's voice. "There are still survivors on Nebula. We have injured. If you can hear this, please respond."

"Davis?"

The message looped, and I realized it was a recording. Hope, if I'd ever managed to feel it, was swept away on a wave of anger, and I wanted to scream. I didn't even know who I was mad at.

Commander Henner for cutting me off. The company for not bothering to search for us. Davis for not being right there.

I had to do something about it.

"Astrid?" The word came back tinny and glitchy, but it was repeated quickly.

"Davis!" I leaned forward so fast I nearly toppled over the desk and Zyrus had to put a stabilizing arm around me.

"You're alive? Truly?" Even through the distance, I could hear the relief. "What's going on?"

"I hoped you could tell me something." Of course, they were just as clueless as I was down on Nebula, maybe even more so. "I've been trying to talk to station security, but they told me you were in quarantine."

"That's ridiculous. No one's sick. They've been flying patrols overhead every day, but no one's come down to get us out of here. They definitely know we're here, we've tried to flag them down for days. I've been trying to get someone on comms, but I could swear they're jamming the signal." Frustration laced his every word.

"How is everyone? Prepped for winter? Any updates?" I'd been a leader of these people for the better part of a decade and knew just how harsh the cold months could be. We didn't lose people to the cold every year, but it happened. And with hope of rescue dangling in front of them, preparations had to be more bitter than normal.

"It's not good, Astrid. We have injured from the fight with the smugglers and the medkits we scavenged from the ruins can only do so much. Plus, we have the people who were forced to work that mine, and you know how it rips you up if you don't have safety equipment. If someone doesn't come get us soon, I think people might start taking drastic action."

My stomach curdled at the thought of my people risking themselves like that. "How low are those surveillance ships flying?"

"Low enough. Tell me the truth. Are they just going to let us rot?"

"I won't let them. Give me a little more time. I promise I will get you guys out of there. Maybe it's time this story spread beyond Nebula Outpost."

The line crackled and popped, but Davis was still there. "I'll try and keep the comms open. Keep me updated." He ended the call.

I wanted to try again, to see if I could talk to anyone else down there and get an even bigger picture, but Davis had said more than enough.

Zyrus led me silently back to my room, seeming to understand that I needed time to process everything.

Back in my room, the door slid shut behind me, and I leaned against it, heaving a big sigh. Zyrus turned to face me, his expression so serious it made something in me hurt.

What had happened to that smiling man I'd met all those years ago? Had I just conjured that up?

He stared at me, eyes dark and deep, and I took a slow, measured step towards him.

He didn't back up.

It was only when I was this close to him, in touching distance, that I realized how tall he was. Usually, I hated to be towered over, but something about him made me feel protected.

"Thank you," I said, and it was for far more than the message to Davis.

He nodded once but said nothing.

Slowly, I raised my hand to his cheek and pressed my palm to his skin. His nostrils flared, and his eyes flashed red, but he remained as still as a statue.

I had to rise up to meet him, and then our lips met. It was soft and tentative, like the ghost of a memory. But Zyrus kissed me back, his hand wrapping around the back of my head and his tongue sweeping into my mouth to claim me.

This was real.

My blood roared in my ears as the kiss went on.

And then Zyrus made a noise in the back of his throat and crashed to the ground at my feet.

10

ZYRUS

M‌Y EYES FLASHED OPEN, ready for the threat.

But there was no threat, only Astrid looming over me, her eyes wide with worry, her hands pressed firmly against my chest. "What the hell was that?" she demanded, her voice laced with a mixture of concern and urgency as she clutched the fabric of my shirt tightly.

I was lying on the ground, my body aching. The last thing I remembered was Astrid's lips pressed against mine, the silken taste of her even better than the memories I'd lived with for the past eleven years.

I reached for her, my body commanding me to take another taste, to continue exactly where we'd left off until all that I knew was her. The warmth of her lips still lingered, igniting a desperate need to reconnect, to recapture that fleeting moment of perfection.

Astrid scrambled up to her feet, out of kissing range.

Very well.

I stood, the world momentarily blurring at the edges as I fought to maintain my balance. "What happened?" I asked as I tried to figure out just how I'd gone from kissing my mate to lying unconscious on the floor.

"What happened!" Her eyes were wide, arms gesticulating. "We kissed for three seconds, and then you passed out like you'd been shot! I thought someone snuck into my room and attacked you. Are you sick? What's going on?"

I hadn't kissed a woman in eleven years. My memory might have been a bit rusty, but unconsciousness had never been part of the process before. The sensation was disorienting, as if my body had short-circuited from the intensity of that brief connection.

"I'm not sick," I insisted, though my voice wavered slightly. My mind felt ... different. It was as if pinpricks of pain and bursts of something indescribable were waking it back up after years of dormancy. A flood of sensations and that had been asleep for so long now surged within me. Despite the confusion and the oddity of it all, I was certain—this was no illness.

"Maybe you should sit down. Let me get you something to drink." She pointed towards the couch with a look on her face that meant arguing was futile.

My mate wanted to fuss over me. I would let her.

She came back with a glass of water that was fizzing with something. "It's a vitamin supplement. It can't hurt."

I drank. The citrusy flavor was an explosion on my tongue, but I ignored it as best as I could, my soulless training kicking in. There was always a fear among our superiors that strong flavors, scents, or other stimulus could set us off, though I'd never heard of a soulless Detyen descending into madness because his meal supplements tasted like something other than sawdust.

"I'm fine," I insisted. More than fine.

I wanted.

From the moment I saw her, I knew that I *should* want Astrid, but now I could see just how feeble that was. It was nearly a physical sensation now, something tugging deep within me and demanding that I reach for her, that I do what it took to take her, to taste her, to keep her.

"Your eyes turned red," she said. She sat in a chair across from me, as if she feared sitting closer might lead to something else.

If she was close enough to touch, I wouldn't resist. I wouldn't even try.

"That happens sometimes." But not to the soulless. When Detyens felt extreme emotions, our eyes could turn red. When our emotions died, we lost the ability to do it.

In the presence of my mate, my emotions were reawakening.

"What's going on, Zyrus?"

It was another opportunity to tell her about our past and who she was to me. But with my newly awakening emotions came something else: doubt. Would she believe me? Could she possibly understand what this meant? What if she didn't want a mate?

"I want to kiss you again." I couldn't bring myself to give her the truth, but I could tell her this.

"Absolutely not. Either you have some weird fainting space disease, or kissing me caused you to pass out. We're not experimenting with that. You should go to medical and get checked out." Her expression was fierce and worried.

"I don't need medical." It had never been spoken between my soulless brethren and I, but we did our best to avoid the medical department. If news of our lives here reached the Detyen Legion and they cared enough to come looking, we'd be dead. It wasn't worth the risk when we could mostly treat ourselves.

She looked ready to argue, but then she shook her head and muttered something I couldn't quite make out. Possibly *men*. "Then get some sleep. If you pass out on me again, I'll drag you to the doctor myself."

I didn't want to go to work. Strange. Every shift that I'd ever scheduled had simply been something I knew I had to do, but today I walked there with a healthy dose of reluctance.

My allotted days off were running low, and if I wanted to keep my job, I needed to show up for a few shifts. No one had tried to attack Astrid in the last few days, and she'd promised to keep to her quarters and contact the others if she needed to leave.

I wanted to stay and guard her. It mattered far more than any shift in the janitorial department could.

But Astrid had insisted she would be fine and perhaps the space would be good for her. In the last two days, she'd looked at me as if I might fall to pieces if we so much as brushed up against each other.

All I wanted to do was kiss her again.

It had consumed my thoughts. And my dreams. No longer was I consumed by the memory of our meeting so long ago. Now all I could imagine was our future and what it might bring.

If she could let me near her.

The shift went by quickly, even with my desire to leave. Feelings were strange. I didn't know how I'd forgotten that, but as I dealt with them, the thought circled my mind.

Every minute dragged into eternity when I wasn't thinking of Astrid. But thoughts of her could make the day pass by in moments. Then I'd remember she was back in her quarters and nowhere near me, and it would stretch unbearably again.

I didn't like this.

But after interminable hours, I was heading back, determined to show her that I was as healthy as ever and prove that one kiss would not take me down.

I didn't realize I was being followed until I was halfway to Astrid's room, my mind still preoccupied with thoughts of her. Then the back of my neck prickled with awareness, a sensation I'd grown to trust over my years as a warrior. I slowed my pace, focusing my senses, and realized that someone in an ill-fitting maintenance uniform was creeping several meters behind me, their footsteps barely audible in the quiet corridor.

I could lose them easily enough; I knew every nook and cranny of this outpost. But my body was aching for activity after hours of forced inaction, muscles tense and ready. A fight would be better than nothing, I reasoned.

I would have reveled in this once, but that part of me was still deadened, still sleeping. I laid in wait with soulless silence, and when my pursuer turned a blind corner, I pounced.

If I expected an easy fight, I was sorely mistaken. He punched out with surprising speed and precision, landing a solid blow to my side that had me grunting in pain and momentarily winded.

Then it was on, a flurry of movement in the dimly lit corridor. I ducked and dodged, my body remembering old training with no need to think about it. I managed to deliver a sharp blow to the side of my attacker's knee that made him stagger—a small victory. But he recovered quickly, going right back at it with renewed vigor. He tripped me up with a swift leg sweep, sending me stumbling and reminding me that I was years out of practice, my movements rusty compared to his fluid grace.

But I couldn't back down, my pride and survival instinct kicking in with equal force. I regained my footing, fists clenched and muscles coiled, ready for the next exchange.

So did he, his stance mirroring mine, a testament to his determination. The air crackled with tension as we circled each other.

I refused to lose.

And so did he.

We were in a public corridor, the stark metal walls and harsh lighting a reminder of our place. Station security could come running at any moment.

My opponent got in a lucky shot that sent me

right to my knees. The impact reverberated through my body, and before I could gather my wits to get up, he smoothly pulled his own blaster from its holster. With practiced ease, he aimed and shot, the energy bolt hitting me square in the chest.

The pain took a moment to bloom, a brief instant of numbness before agony exploded through every nerve ending. Then it was all consuming, a white-hot fire that spread from my chest to the tips of my fingers and toes. I couldn't move my limbs if I tried, my body refusing to respond as the paralyzing effects of the blast took hold. All I could do was lie there, gasping for breath, as the world around me began to blur.

Was this it? Had I failed so quickly?

Astrid.

I had to get to my mate.

She was in danger.

But my attacker knew he had me, and he hooked his arms under my boneless shoulders and dragged me a few meters down the hall to a recessed alcove. He pressed a button on the wall, and a chute opened.

He dumped me in, and I landed with a thick thump in a foul-smelling soup of food waste.

Then the walls started closing in as the compactor came to life.

11
ZYRUS

THE DOOR CLOSED with an echoing clang, plunging the whole area into complete darkness. The smell was overwhelming, enough to make me gag and nearly vomit up whatever I'd eaten for lunch. But after only a few moments, it began to dissipate as my body adjusted to the stench.

I couldn't die down here.

There was a constant, low-frequency hum permeating the air, accompanied by the unsettling sensation of food waste shifting and churning around me, gradually getting closer. The agitator was in full swing, its mechanical arms methodically separating the salvageable waste from the rest. The former would be compacted and repurposed, while the latter was destined for the fiery maw of the incinerator.

Time was running out. I needed to move, or I'd be crushed into oblivion along with the rest of the discarded matter. But the darkness rendered me blind, unable to navigate or formulate an escape plan. There were emergency lights installed somewhere in this disgusting chamber, but I had no way to engage them while submerged in the sea of muck. My fingers, slick with who-knows-what, groped uselessly in the darkness.

Even though there was no one to hear me, I yelled for help, my voice echoing off the unseen walls of the chamber. My burgeoning emotions screamed at me to find a way out, but logic told me to conserve energy. But I couldn't help but shout again, desperation creeping into my tone. Every system on Nebula Outpost had redundant safety features, I reminded myself. People weren't supposed to end up in these things, but accidents happened. That's why there were fail-safes.

The compactor kept churning relentlessly, the low hum growing louder, and the area around me remained stubbornly dark. I could feel the vibrations through the sludge surrounding me, a constant reminder that time was running out.

I had to find a way out, and fast.

I wasn't panicking. My heart rate was elevated from the fight, but not by much. Even with my emotions coming back to me, they weren't strong enough to overcome my training.

And that training was simple. Assess. Adapt. Execute.

I needed to get out of this compactor and back to Astrid before my attacker could get to her. I had no doubt she'd be the next target. It made sense. Take out the guard first and then grab the true target when there was little resistance. The thought of Astrid in danger sent a fresh wave of determination through me, pushing back against the oppressive stench of refuse.

A spike of pain lanced my chest, sharp and unexpected. I looked down instinctively, even though I could see nothing in the blackness. Instead, I reached and felt for something, anything that might explain the sudden discomfort. My fingers probed through the sludge, but there was nothing there. No wound, no foreign object.

Ah. Yes. This was panic. The realization hit me with a jolt. This unfamiliar sensation, this tightness in my chest, the quickening of my breath—it was fear. Not for myself, trapped in this mechanical maw, but for Astrid. The emotion, forgotten and unwelcome, threatened to overwhelm me. But I couldn't let it. I needed to stay focused, to find a way out. Astrid was counting on me, whether she knew it or not.

Astrid was my only thought and my only weakness. If I let her consume my mind, I'd never get out of the compactor.

I had to push her aside, just for now. And it hurt. But I was no good to her if I was crushed into a square of meat and blood and recycled back into the station's food processors.

I needed light.

If I could see, I might spot my escape. But I had no way to trigger the emergency light from where I stood. The current was getting stronger, and my time was running out.

But I was wearing my work uniform and that had small lights embedded in the collar so I could work in dark spaces and keep my hands free.

I reached up and pinched each light, ignoring the squelch of wet fabric and trying to suppress the urge to gag as a fresh wave of odor assaulted my nostrils. The stench was so potent I could taste it, and I had to breathe through my mouth to avoid retching.

This place was a nightmare of filth and decay. As I stood there, knee-deep in the muck, a disturbing thought crossed my mind. Did so much of this really get recycled into our food? I worked in the janitorial department and had seen my fair share of messes, but this was on another level entirely. It was better not to dwell on how some things on the station were made, especially not when I was literally swimming in the raw materials.

Twin beams of light pierced the darkness, illuminating the space immediately in front of me. It wasn't much, barely enough to see a meter ahead, but it proved my eyes were functional. The dim glow revealed swirling patterns of sludge and debris, bits of unidentifiable matter floating past. I squinted, trying to make out any details that might help me escape this death trap.

Assess.

The inside of the compactor was full of waste and bits of debris from whatever had been thrown in before me. But there was a panel on the far wall, above the muck and just out of reach if I stood under it.

If there was any kind of control in that panel, any kind of safety override, I might just get out of there and get back to my mate.

But moving through the muck and the current was harder than anticipated. The watery sludge sucked at my feet and pushed me back with more force than I expected, and every few steps I crashed into something too big to kick aside and nearly went plunging into the muck.

It felt like there was something living beneath my feet, a giant beast hell bent on keeping me in place until it could decide exactly what I was and what it wanted to do with me.

It was just machinery, just an old system that kept the station running, but in the dim with only myself to rely on, I couldn't banish the thought.

Adapt.

I changed my pattern, turning from the panel and moving with the swirling current. If I couldn't fight it, I would ride it. The beams of my lights illuminated the bumpy surface of the watery mix, and I tried not to imagine what I was mixed in with.

The edge of the current turned and lead me to the far end of the compactor, close enough to the wall that my fingers nearly brushed it.

A moment later, they did brush it, but I hadn't moved.

The walls were still pushing in slowly, the ever-decreasing space making the current stronger as debris and waste were separated.

I had to fight the current once more, unwilling to let myself be carried in another circle. It was too much of a risk. I'd been in there too long already.

Execute.

I spotted the panel once more, and it was just as far out of reach as I'd predicted. But there was a pile of something in the muck, and I climbed, not letting myself worry about whether or not it would hold my weight.

My fingers brushed the edge of the panel, and I pressed down, hoping for a pressure release door.

The door sprang open, and there was only one large button inside. The emergency stop.

I pressed it and winced as a giant screeching assaulted my ears followed by the unmistakable blaring of an emergency alarm. Someone would be here to check on me in no time; they'd get me out.

And then they'd ask questions, they'd detain me and demand to know how I'd ended up in the compactor and what mischief I'd been up to.

Astrid would still be in danger.

I couldn't wait for a rescue.

But I couldn't see a way out.

12

ASTRID

Zyrus's shift had ended more than an hour ago, but he hadn't come home. Or, well, back to my place. I should have been jumping for joy at the hours spent alone, but instead, worry nagged at me.

Where was he?

I tried to call his comm, but he didn't answer. I was tempted to call the station line to his department but resisted the urge. I wasn't some nagging wife who got to make demands about where he was. He'd get there when he got there.

But what if something was wrong?

I could call one of the Detyens. They might know. He shared his room with a man named

Thalor. Perhaps he'd just gone back to pick up some things. Or maybe Ryklin or Drex could help.

Or maybe I was freaking out because I was convinced there was danger lurking around every corner, and I'd finally had the space to really process that fear.

I didn't like it. Not one bit.

I stood, but then I hesitated. I'd promised to stick to my quarters with Zyrus out at work. Someone had been following me the last time I went rogue. He had a point.

But he wasn't *there*.

Screw it.

I was just going to walk the same path he would have taken to work. If I ran into him, great, he could ream me out for going back on my promise. If not, well, I'd figure it out from there.

I missed the forest. I never thought I could, especially not only a few weeks out from the monotony of being trapped there forever. But the space station was loud in all the wrong ways, the smells antiseptic and sometimes a bit dusty. It all felt so artificial.

And there was no sign of Zyrus. Something deep in my gut was pulling me forward, as if I had a sort of sixth sense that would allow me to find him. Which was ludicrous. We weren't even the same species. Nothing in the millions of years of evolution that had led to me should have anything to do with him.

Not that I was an expert in astrobiology.

"Hey!"

I turned around at the noise and had only a second to react to the blaster in the stranger's hand. I dove to the floor as he shot, and the blast went over my head, close enough to singe my hair.

Zyrus was going to kill me.

But there was no time to think about my Detyen as my attacker lined up for a second shot. His hand was unsteady, shaking as he tried to level the blaster, and I reached out and grasped the thin leg of a chair set up against the wall and jerked it his way. From where I was lying on the floor, I didn't have much leverage, but he shot the ceiling, and then his blaster went flying.

I launched myself off the floor and sprinted three steps before he was on me, tackling me to the floor, hand wrapped in my hair and holding me in place.

I struggled. I bucked my hips, I bit at him when he was stupid enough to put his fingers near my mouth, and I screamed with all the volume I could manage.

It didn't help.

There was a light directly overhead, and it was bright enough to blind me just enough so I couldn't make out my attacker's face.

Was this how I died?

During those dark days after the explosion, when we'd finally given up hope of a rescue, I'd been certain we wouldn't last for long. I'd stared down death with the kind of defiance that only a twenty-three-year-old could muster. Now, as my attacker got his hands around my throat, that naive defiance was gone.

I tried to grasp his thumbs, to break the harsh grip he had, but that only made my vision get fuzzier, as if I was helping him to choke me.

Zyrus, I'm sorry. We could have had so much more.

I fought it as my vision went gray around the edges. I bucked and twisted, desperate to stop him.

And then he was gone.

I coughed and spluttered as air rushed back into my lungs and the world came rushing back. There was someone standing over me, but it wasn't my attacker.

It was Zyrus.

A nasty smell emanated from him, and his

clothes were soaked. His eyes glowed red, and were those claws?

He had claws. Holy shit.

Zyrus got his hand around the throat of my attacker and squeezed, claws scraping against gentle skin, not quite hard enough to make him bleed.

The man whimpered and squirmed while he clutched at Zyrus's hand and tried to free himself. I felt a sick sense of satisfaction. Now he knew what it felt like.

I raised a hand to my neck. It was warm and tender. I'd be bruised later, and I was beyond grateful for the air I could pull in now, even if it burned going down.

"You're going to talk," Zyrus informed him, his voice deadly calm.

The man made a sputtering sound that might have been assent.

"Not in the hallway." My voice was scratchy, and it hurt to talk, but I did my best to ignore it. "Station security could be here any minute."

Zyrus titled his head to the side, considering it. Then he lowered the man enough so that his feet scraped against the ground. "There's a door labeled Authorized Personnel Only. Type in 029093X into the keypad." He nodded towards the door and dragged the man after me.

My hands shook a tiny bit as I did as instructed. This was a side of Zyrus I'd never seen before. It went beyond cold to the edge of something cruel. I didn't like it. He was my protector, not my avenger. I didn't want him giving up pieces of his soul for me.

But we needed answers.

Zyrus dragged the man inside and gave me a look. "Maybe you should go back to your room."

"I'm not leaving you." If this was a side of him, I had to see it. And a part of me wanted to. The man dangling in Zyrus's grip had nearly killed me. A bit of payback wouldn't be terrible.

He nodded. "Get me a chair and something to tie his hands."

We were in a room that looked like a mix between a large utility closet and a small office. There was a desk and two chairs wedged into a corner, and the walls were hung with various cleaning and repair implements.

Or torture devices.

Now was not the time to let my imagination run wild.

I pulled one of the chairs over to Zyrus and then grabbed some cording off the wall that looked like it was meant to tie down furniture or tarps. Zyrus took it and efficiently tied the man to the chair. He didn't warn him not to run, and the man was too defeated to try.

"What's your name?" he asked.

The man glared and spat at Zyrus's feet. Well, he tried to. A bit of spittle flicked out of his mouth, but it landed on his chin.

Zyrus waited, not asking again. And after several long moments, the man began to breathe heavily and shift in his seat. "It's Yoree." Yoree's shoulders sank as he answered.

"Why did you attack me and Astrid?" his voice was so even that it scared me just a little, and I wasn't the one being interrogated. I stayed a little behind Yoree, more interested in watching Zyrus than the bound man.

"She was just there. I took the opportunity. I thought you were gone, and this was all over."

Gone? As in *gone*? Dead? I sucked in a sharp breath, and Zyrus shot a glance my way. He gave a minute shake of his head. Whatever happened, he didn't need me bringing it up now.

But I'd definitely bring it up later.

"*What* was all over?" He was angry beyond anything I'd ever seen. I wasn't sure how I knew that. His tone didn't change. But his body had tightened, and his eyes were still that sinister, alluring red. "Tell me what's been going on. From the beginning."

"I don't even know, man! Some guy sent me a bunch of credits to keep an eye on the girl and scare her a bit. Then he paid me more to separate the two of you. Told me to do it however I saw fit. Then you attacked me, and we were right by the food compactor. It made sense! Nothing personal." Zyrus stepped closer, and Yoree flinched back.

I was still caught on the idea of the food compactor.

"Who hired you?"

"I don't know! It was all through the messaging system. The credits showed up, so I didn't ask too many questions." There were tears in his eyes now, his face all scrunched up in fear or pain. Maybe both.

"When did this person hire you?" Zyrus didn't move any closer.

"Like three weeks ago, maybe. Not long after she got on the station. The messages come from a relay account, someone off station. I tried to track them; I'm not an idiot."

Zyrus made a humming noise. "And what's your job when you're not stalking innocent women?"

Yoree shrugged—or tried to. It wasn't easy with his hands tied behind his back. "Station security."

I didn't mean to, but I made a noise. Station security again. "Was he the person that was following me earlier? Or the person who attacked us that day?"

Zyrus didn't answer me. Instead, he said, "I think you should step outside now."

Yoree shook his head violently and looked over at me, eyes wide. "Don't leave me alone with him."

That plea almost got me to walk out. But if I walked out, Zyrus would kill him. I could see it in the way he was holding himself. He had the man's blaster tucked in his belt, and his claws were still out, a clear threat. I nodded for him to come closer to me, and for a moment, I thought he'd resist, but he joined me in the corner.

We took a few steps back to get completely out of Yoree's sight.

"Don't kill him," I said. I tried not to make it sound like I was begging. I wouldn't plea for the man's life. This wasn't about him.

"He tried to kill you." Zyrus was breathing hard, and I wanted to gather him into my arms and hold him close.

Instead, I reached up and brushed my fingers

along his cheek. "He's more scared of you than whoever is paying him. Use it. You know computers. Have him send the messages to you. More violence won't solve this."

"It will keep you safe." He was resolute.

I gripped his hand, claws and all. "Whoever hired him will just hire someone else. *Was* this the person you saw following me earlier?"

He shook his head. "No, that was a woman."

"Then put the fear of *you* into him and let him go. You don't need more blood on your hands."

"Scaring him will still involve blood."

"Then you don't need more death." Zyrus was a warrior, a former one anyway, but he wasn't a murderer. And if we could avoid it, I didn't want him killing. I hoped I wasn't making a mistake.

"You should leave the room now," he said. His look was grave. "I won't kill him. And I'll join you in your quarters shortly."

Could I trust him to do what he said?

I turned around and left the room.

13
ASTRID

I SHOWERED. And waited.

Then waited some more.

Visions of Yoree somehow slipping free of his restraints and overpowering Zyrus assaulted me, twisting my stomach into knots. My mind raced with worst-case scenarios until I felt physically ill. I paced the small room, cursing myself for leaving Zyrus alone with that monster. What if something had gone wrong?

But an eternity later—or an hour or two—the door finally slid open. Zyrus marched in, his face an impassive mask of nothingness. Even when his eyes met mine, I couldn't read a single emotion. It was like looking at a stranger, and I desperately wanted to know what had happened to make him retreat back behind that cold façade. Except I was pretty sure I did know. And I didn't need to know any more about it.

"He'll live," Zyrus stated flatly, his voice devoid of inflection.

"Yes." I wouldn't have walked away if I didn't trust him. And if he was lying to me, whatever there was between us could never be more than a flicker of possibility.

Zyrus headed straight for the shower without saying another word. I had questions about how he'd ended up in a waste compactor smelling like rotten food and worse, but now wasn't the time. Whatever he'd just done, he needed to get his head on straight. I wasn't going to make it worse.

The water ran for a long time. The seemingly eternal hot water was my favorite thing about Nebula Outpost. I'd bathed in a river for a decade, I'd missed the luxury of steam.

Eventually, it shut off, and I realized I'd been sitting and doing no more than listening to the water run the entire time. I stood and grabbed a plate and cup sitting on the table beside me, tidying up.

I turned around, and Zyrus emerged from the

bathroom wearing nothing but a towel, drops of water clinging to his bare chest. His scars were more visible now, little nicks and scratches that had healed poorly over the years and the dark marks that covered his teal skin in a random pattern. I wanted to trace them with my fingertips and learn every story behind each mark.

But first I had to say something. Or I should.

Zyrus was looking at me, frozen where he stood. His teal skin glistened with moisture, muscles tense beneath the surface. He had some clothes in a drawer in the bedroom; it would only take him a minute to change, but he stayed put. The air between us felt charged, heavy with unspoken words.

"Are you okay?" I finally asked, my voice barely above a whisper. The question was inadequate, but I needed to break the silence.

Zyrus's eyes flickered, a hint of something raw behind them. "I don't think I'm the one anyone needs to worry about," he said, his tone flat but with an edge of bitterness. The words hung in the air, laden with implications about what had transpired with Yoree.

"I always worry about you." The words tumbled out before I could stop them, more of a confession than I'd intended. I let them hang in the air between us, my heart pounding. Then my gaze fell to his hands, and I noticed the angry red swelling across his knuckles. Without thinking, I reached out and gently took his hand in mine, bringing it closer to inspect the damage. The skin was mottled with fresh bruises, and I tried not to imagine how he'd gotten them. For me. Because of what I'd let him do.

"Do you need healing gel?" I asked softly, my throat tight. I didn't want to think about what had caused these marks, how he'd inflicted this pain on himself for my sake. The weight of it settled in my chest, a mix of guilt and something deeper I wasn't ready to name.

"They'll heal," Zyrus replied, his voice low and rough. "But thank you." He didn't pull away. Instead, he held my hand, his larger one engulfing mine. I felt the calluses on his fingers as he began to trace my palm with his thumb, the gentle motion at odds with the violence those hands had just committed. The contrast made me shiver.

My heart was beating too fast, and I couldn't quite catch my breath. I remembered what had happened the last time we kissed—the way fear had crashed over me when Zyrus went limp.

But I couldn't pull away.

And I didn't want to.

I held his hand up and brushed my lips against his bruises, something more tender than a kiss, more tentative. The warmth of his skin against my mouth sent a shiver through me. I could taste the faint metallic tang of blood, reminding me of the violence he'd endured—and inflicted.

His thumb slid over the pulse in my wrist, caressing my skin. The gentle motion contrasted sharply with the raw evidence of what his hands were capable of. My breath caught as his touch ignited a spark that raced through my veins.

"Astrid ..." His voice was rough and low, a mix of desire and hesitation that made my name sound like both a prayer and a curse. I couldn't tell if he was warning me off or trying to coax me closer. The uncertainty hung between us, thick and heady. I swallowed hard, torn between the urge to step back and the overwhelming desire to close what little distance remained.

I tilted my head up to look at him, my neck craning to meet his gaze. He towered over me, his broad frame dwarfing mine. I was surprised by how much I liked that, how it made me feel protected and safe in a way I hadn't experienced in years. The realization sent a shiver down my spine. My voice was barely above a whisper when I asked, "What do you want, Zyrus?"

His eyes darkened to red, pupils dilating as they locked onto mine. The air between us seemed to crackle with tension. After a heartbeat that felt like an eternity, he answered, his voice low and rough with need.

"You."

Before I could process his response, he leaned down, one hand coming up to cup my cheek. His touch was surprisingly gentle for someone so powerful. I felt his warm breath against my skin a split second before his lips brushed mine. The contact was feather-light, almost hesitant, but it sent sparks racing through my body.

I was the one that deepened the kiss, sliding my tongue against his mouth and letting him open for me. Heat rolled through me, something raw and primal that I'd only ever felt with him.

It scared me.

But I'd be lying if I said I didn't want more.

He wrapped his arm around me and drew me flush against him, heat searing me wherever we touched. It was everything I wanted and everything I was terrified of all at once.

Zyrus was strong enough to crush me, he had

claws that could tear me apart, but I trusted him with my life, with my very soul. And I wanted him more than I'd ever wanted anything.

He lifted me up as if I weighed nothing, and I wrapped my legs around his waist, never breaking our kiss. There was nothing tentative about this now, and he was as steady as ever. If he passed out again, I didn't know what I'd do, but I couldn't stop.

He carried me to the bed and laid me down, stretching out above me. His towel fell away at some point, but I couldn't get a good look. There didn't need to be a rush. We could take our time.

But my body wanted more. Demanded everything.

Zyrus's fingers played at the hem of my shirt, and I helped him tug it over my head. Then he took a moment to just *look* at me, nostrils flaring and eyes going that demonic red. I shivered under his gaze.

I loved how he looked at me, as if I was something precious. Something he needed to claim.

He leaned down and kissed me again, exploring my mouth with his tongue, and then moving to my jaw and my neck. His teeth scraped my skin, and I couldn't stop the moan that slipped out.

I arched under him, grasping his shoulders and holding him close. I never wanted him to let me go.

He kissed a path down my collarbone and then to my breasts, taking one in his mouth and sucking on my nipple until I writhed beneath him.

I tangled my fingers in his hair and pulled him up for another kiss. I didn't want him to stop, but I wanted *more*. My pants and underwear went next, and then I was completely naked before him.

I felt bold and powerful.

Cherished.

Zyrus stared down at me with a reverence that stole my breath. "You're beautiful," he whispered.

I reached down between us and wrapped my hand around his cock, stroking him from root to tip. This didn't feel like something new; instead, it felt like we'd been waiting forever and now, *finally*, we were where we were supposed to be.

He groaned and thrust into my grip, eyes closed and face tense with pleasure. I wanted to taste him, to make him feel as good as he made me feel. But not yet. I kept stroking him, teasing him until he gasped and pulled back.

He cursed under his breath and then grabbed my thighs, spreading my legs wide for him. His fingers teased my slit, dipping inside me and then circling my swollen flesh until I was panting and arching off the bed.

"Please, Zyrus," I begged.

He moved over me, lining himself up with my entrance. "Look at me." The demand wasn't something I'd dream of resisting.

I did as he asked, meeting his red gaze and losing myself in his eyes. Then he pushed inside me, filling me with one long stroke that made me gasp and moan.

He stayed still for a moment, giving me time to adjust. And then he started to move, thrusting into me with a steady rhythm that stoked the fire burning inside me higher and brighter.

I clung to him, digging my nails into his back and urging him on.

It felt like something more than physical was tying us together, a bond reaching out from him to me, anchoring itself deep in my chest, never to be undone.

I felt wild and free and unbreakable.

Zyrus picked up his pace, fucking me harder, hitting a spot inside me that made me see stars. I cried out, my body tightening around him as I spiraled higher and higher towards the edge of the universe.

And then I tipped over, waves of pleasure rolling through me. Zyrus groaned and followed me, filling me with hot spurts of his seed as he came.

It was perfect. Everything I could possibly want.

Until Zyrus's eyes rolled back into his head, blood trickled out of his nose, and he collapsed, weightless, on top of me.

14
ZYRUS

THE BED WAS soft beneath me, a warm comfort on aching muscles and an even stronger aching head. I hadn't thought of my own comfort waking any morning for years.

And I wasn't in my own bed.

Astrid was perched above me, face frantic and a little ... angry? It was difficult to read her expression, but not nearly as difficult as it should have been.

Denya.

The recognition bloomed once more, an old friend I'd been desperate to recognize for so long, and now I did. The certainty lay heavy in my chest, and I had no idea how I'd ever forgotten.

"What the hell is going on, Zyrus? Are you dying?" She clutched my shoulder as if she was afraid to let go. "Why do you keep passing out?" She looked down at her own hand and released me like I was burning her. Or perhaps the other way around.

"Denya." I had spent so long keeping the thought to myself that there was no way I could keep it from escaping now. It burst out of me, a vicious animal eager to pounce or a flower ready to bloom. I sat up, head spinning just a little. I tasted the tang of blood in my mouth.

All of it was inconsequential next to the woman beside me.

"What are you—"

I cut her off with a kiss, pain dissolving into pleasure with the brush of her tongue. Our bodies were still naked, and mine was ready for more, desperate after so long without. But Astrid pulled back, her chest heaving.

I stared, unable to tear my gaze away. I'd known she was beautiful. Gorgeous. Mine. But now that knowledge was visceral, a primal urge burning low in my gut that had my eyes roaming hungrily over her body. I traced the curve of her hips, the swell of her breasts, places I hadn't dared to consider in far too long. My mouth went dry as I drank her in, committing every detail to memory.

"My face is up here, buddy," Astrid said, her tone

sharp but with an undercurrent I couldn't quite place. Amusement? Desire?

I snapped my gaze to hers. Did I blush? I felt no shame in appreciating my mate. But I *felt*. So much. Everything. And I wanted more.

"I thought I remembered, but it's so much more." I reached for her, my hand covering her side, sliding around her waist, her skin so soft and delicate. And mine. After so long, she was finally mine. "You changed my life the first time I saw you."

Under my hand, she stiffened and pulled away, ever so slightly. Her face was shrouded in something it was still too difficult to read. Anger? Fear? Confusion?

Guilt?

If anyone should feel guilty, it was me.

"I should have said something weeks ago. But I ... There's so much to say." I hadn't been nervous like this in so long that I barely knew how to deal with it. My heart raced, and my palms felt clammy. Words I'd held back for years threatened to spill out all at once, but I struggled to organize my thoughts.

"Why did you pass out? Let's deal with that first. I think you need to go to medical." She pulled the sheet up to cover her nakedness, as if I might be tempted to do something if she continued to sit there bare. The soft rustle of fabric against skin seemed unnaturally loud in the tense silence between us. I caught a whiff of her scent—a mix of sweat and something uniquely her—as she shifted away from me. The distance felt like a chasm, despite our physical proximity.

As if a sheet could quell my desire.

"I don't need medical." It came out harsh. Agitated. These newly awakened emotions were hard to deal with, all knotted up and unable to be ignored. "I have my soul back, that's what happened."

"Your soul? What are you talking about?"

She didn't know. Of course not. I hadn't told her, and why would anyone else? I wanted to rush into this, to declare for anyone to hear that Astrid was mine and that I was hers. But now was not the time. She had to understand.

It came out in a rush. "Detyens die at the age of thirty if we don't find our mates. However, the Detyen Legion has a procedure they can perform that prevents that. The only cost is our emotions. We call it a soul. Until Drex found Pippa, none of us here thought there was anything beyond that existence. But then he started to feel again. Then Ryklin. And now ..."

"You." She didn't move any closer. "But we met before. Why did you ...?"

"You remember?" No, that wasn't what we were focusing on right now. "We met. We kissed. But I didn't ... claim you. I spent every moment I could searching for you until I was banished from the Legion. Even after I lost my soul, I looked for you. You've—"

Her eyes widened. "Banished?"

"That's why we're all here. We did not fit the expected role of soulless warriors. Rather than kill us, we all had someone who cared enough to help us escape."

"They would have *killed* you?" Now she did lean in closer, but she stopped herself before she touched me.

Right, this was not something normal to someone who hadn't lived in the Legion. I simply nodded. I had no reason to defend them. "Do you remember our meeting? I thought you must not have. I recognized you from the first."

She leaned back and looked away. "I didn't, not at first. But it's been coming back. Why didn't you mention anything?"

I didn't know how to answer that. It would have made logical sense to mention the meeting, to let her know who she was to me from the moment we met again. But it hadn't *felt* right, even if I couldn't yet feel. "I didn't want to scare you away. I thought that if you knew, you might not want me to guard you."

"That's not a good reason to say nothing!" She threw the sheet off and got out of bed, picking up clothes and throwing them on haphazardly. Her shirt was on backwards, and she didn't seem to realize it, or she didn't care.

"You're right." I wanted to get out of bed and pull her into my arms, but she was vibrating with energy, possibly anger, and I didn't want to set it off further.

I was beginning to understand this emotion thing.

"But why didn't you say anything either?" If she knew about our meeting, we'd both been keeping secrets. I wasn't angry about it. Once she saw that, she would calm down. It was only logical.

"Because I thought I was going crazy. I wasn't going to tell you about my random sex dreams!"

"I want you to tell me everything about them." Now I did get out of bed, fully naked and unashamed. Astrid may have been angry, but she wasn't blind, and her eyes raked over me.

My cock liked that.

All of me did.

"This is crazy, Zyrus. Stay right there." She shot a hand out and pointed to my feet, as if casting a magical spell to hold me in place.

I froze.

"We kissed, and you passed out. We fucked, and you passed out. What if we do more and something worse happens? This is—we need to take a minute to figure it out. A long minute. A while. I can't be responsible for hurting you."

She cared. It was a frustrating kind of care that meant I couldn't hold her in my arms and soothe her the way I wanted most, but as my denya wished, I could not deny her. Not now.

Not yet.

But I would find a way to have her in my arms again. Soon.

<h1 style="text-align:center">15
ASTRID</h1>

SPACE MADE a hell of a lot of sense when the image of Zyrus lying limp on my bed was fresh in my head. It was harder to remember why I shouldn't touch him when he was going through his daily stretches in the living room, pants slung low and shirt cast aside to show off his chiseled chest.

A chest I could be rubbing myself all over if I just said the word.

He didn't speak to me, but something told me that he knew I was there. Was it the bond between us, that thing I could feel deep in my gut that connected me to him? Or was it something baser? The kind of awareness that only came from realized attraction.

My body was a simmering kettle of need, and I had to ignore it.

But I couldn't stop watching.

Zyrus's body moved smoothly; a liquid grace that hinted at a strength I'd seen up close. He was a warrior, but right now he looked more like an artist, a dancer, body fluidly transitioning from one move to the next.

I wanted him so damn badly that it hurt.

But I was afraid. What would happen if it was too much? Could being with me kill him? Would he pass out every time we fucked? How was I supposed to live with that risk?

He bent forward, grasping his arms behind his legs for a moment before slowly rising, his hands fanning out in a wide circle before finally coming to rest at his side. He paused for a moment and then turned to face me. "Did you sleep well?" he asked.

No. I bit the word back. Any release washed away on a wave of anxiety after I banished him from my bed. I'd tossed and turned all night, sneaking out somewhere in the early hours just to make sure he was still breathing. "I'm fine. How about you?"

He took two stalking steps towards me before stopping himself. "It could have been better. If I had you in my arms."

"Zyrus ..." He was close enough to touch, and my hand was on him before I could tell myself to resist. I snapped it back like I'd been burned. "If you won't go to medical, how can I know you're okay?" I couldn't say I liked doctors, but we had a whole medical department at our disposal up there. This wasn't the encampment down on Nebula. If there was a medical problem, we could get answers, or at least try.

"There's nothing wrong with me. Not anymore." He didn't step back.

All I'd have to do was tilt my head up and I could be kissing him. Or I could lean forward and bury my face in his chest and let him carry me off to my room. I just had to stop saying no and I could have everything.

If it was this hard after only a few hours, how impossible would it be to deny him forever?

"How can you know that?" An image flashed in my head, the way his eyes rolled back as he went limp. For a horrible second, I thought he was dead. He'd only been out a few moments, shorter than after the kiss, but long enough. Too long to bear.

He was quiet for a moment, considering. "Drex and Ryklin both went through something similar. I'm no different than them."

"You are to me."

The words hung between us, a declaration, one I couldn't face at that moment.

I spun around and marched to the bathroom, turning on the shower and hoping it would drown out any noise of Zyrus in the main room. If there were tears, they got caught in the spray.

But I couldn't hide in the bathroom forever.

I didn't look into the main room as I went to my bedroom wrapped up in a towel. If I saw the way Zyrus looked at me ... No! No thinking about Zyrus when I was next to naked.

I pulled on clothes and sat on the edge of the bed, elbows resting on my thighs and head cradled in my hands. How was I going to get control of this? Should I talk to Drex or Ryklin? Pippa or Noelle? I barely knew them. Yes, they might have answers, but it felt like asking too much; it was too intimate and too new. And what would they think? Zyrus was supposed to be protecting me, not crawling into my bed.

There was one person I could talk to who'd help me clear my head. She might not know anything about Detyen mating rituals, but she knew *me*, and that was the important part.

Zyrus accompanied me silently down to Alice's

place, and I couldn't resist reaching out and giving his hand a squeeze before I knocked on her door. He took advantage, raising my hand and brushing his lips against my knuckles. I shivered, and he stepped back before it could become anything more.

I was going to go insane.

When I stepped into Alice's room and the door shut behind me, cutting me off from Zyrus and the rest of the station, I leaned back against it and groaned.

Alice raised an eyebrow. "Everything alright?"

I closed my eyes and let my head roll from side to side, my skull still resting against her door.

"Do you want to talk about it?"

I cracked an eye open and shook my head again. Even if that was my whole reason for coming here, now my tongue felt like lead in my mouth. Alice was my lifeline down on Nebula, a person I'd known for more than a decade. But that was the thing—we'd just known each other. I wouldn't call us close friends.

No, they were still stuck on Nebula while I was up here upset that a super hot alien wanted to crawl into my bed for the rest of my life.

I forced myself to stand up properly. And when I really looked around, worry shot through me. The place was a mess. Had it been ransacked? For the millionth time, I wondered if I should have insisted on Alice having someone to watch out for her.

Then I noticed the bag on her bed. Clothes were piled beside it, the outfits she'd managed to acquire in our weeks on Nebula Outpost. "Are you moving to new quarters?" Her room was cramped, definitely, but she hadn't said a word about it being too small.

Alice sank down onto the bed and grinned. "I heard back from Cadence and Namyra. They thought I was trying to scam them at first."

"And you convinced them otherwise?" That was a problem I hadn't thought of. Disbelief, sure. But I'd forgotten how eager some people were to prey on others' grief.

Her smile widened even farther. "Eventually." She picked up a pair of pants and started to carefully fold them. "Cadence said Cassian, our son, just graduated from high school. With honors." The smile faded a bit, and she stuffed the pants into her bag harder than necessary.

"Wow. Little Cassian. Really? And is he a champion speeder race/swimmer/genius like he wanted to be?" Telling stories about our families had been a way to cope in the beginning, and I remembered Alice sharing a lot about her little boy.

"Apparently he's been diving for several years. Off of cliffs." She scowled. "I can't believe Cadence lets him do that."

"Says the woman who did the exact same thing when we found that bend in the river." It had been a day of joy not too long after the explosion, though when Rory hit the water wrong and hurt his ankle, we remembered just how impossible medical care was, trapped as we were.

"Do you think he even remembers me? He was so young when I left. Cadence didn't want me to go, but the money was so good, and my contract was only a year. I thought ..." She let out a huff of air. "Well, what I thought doesn't matter."

"I'm sure he remembers you. Your wife wouldn't let him forget. When do you leave?" With her bags nearly packed, she couldn't be staying long.

"Cadence needs to arrange the ticket, but not long. Make sure to contact me when the lawsuit gets put together. I want to sue these bastards for all they're worth. And then some."

"What makes you think that I'll be the one putting that together?" Though it had been on my mind, something to worry about *after* everyone was safe and far away from Nebula.

"You always take charge. It's just what you do."

She looked at me for several beats. "Now do you want to talk about it?"

"I have no idea how to help everyone down on Nebula." It wasn't why I'd come here, but sitting with Alice was a harsh reminder of everything I'd been whisked away from, of everything I still needed to do.

If only I could figure out how.

"Stop focusing on what you can't do and do what you can." She slipped her hand inside her bag and pulled out a thin tablet, touching the screen to wake it up. She tapped it a few times, and my communicator vibrated. "I've been thinking of strategies. Legal, illegal, and other."

"Other?"

Alice shrugged.

"Maybe that will help. Or maybe it will just help you think. You look so tense you're about to explode. Find a way to loosen up, and things will get better."

That startled a hollow laugh out of me. I stood. "Don't leave without saying goodbye."

"I won't."

Zyrus met me outside of her room and walked me the short path back to mine. There was a really easy way to loosen up, if I was willing to take the risk.

I wasn't.

"I want you to teach me how to defend myself," I said as the door slid closed behind him. "I want to be able to fight off anyone who comes at me."

He considered me for a moment. "A blaster would do that better than anything."

"Do you have one of those sitting around?" I'd shot one before, though it had been a long while. "I haven't exactly seen them in any shop."

"They're restricted to station security, though it should be easy enough to get one on the black market. But not quick."

"Then show me how to defend myself without one." I wasn't waiting around for weapons to magically appear.

Zyrus hesitated for a fraction of a second. "If someone attacks you, you should run. I'm there to defend you."

"And if you're not there?"

"Then I'm dead."

The words were a punch to the gut. I couldn't imagine a galaxy without him in it now that he was so close, now that we'd …

No, not thinking about that.

"Let's imagine a less dire situation where you're somehow incapacitated but not dead and I need to defend myself, okay? You tripped over your feet, and some attacker got the drop on me."

That startled a sound out of him, and it took me a second to realize it was a laugh.

I'd never heard him laugh before.

"I won't trip over my feet."

"Please, Zyrus." I needed to do something, and this was the best idea I had.

Or it seemed that way until he stepped close and clasped my wrist. "What do you do now?" he asked.

Oh, shit.

I gulped and tugged my arm back, but his grip was solid. "You tell me what to do. Come on."

"Self-defense is mostly instinct and improvisation. Try something." He squeezed. It wasn't hard enough to bruise, but it did hurt just a bit.

I rammed my shoulder into his chest then jerked myself back with all my might. And it worked. It freaking worked.

"Ha!" I pointed straight at him, and he grabbed my wrist again.

"When you escape a hold, don't hang around to get caught again." He tugged me towards him, and I tried to twist away.

But I couldn't get free.

We ended up pressed together, his grip on my

wrists tightening as he pinned me against him. Heat radiated off him, and my breath hitched.

He stared down at me, nostrils flaring. "Do you want me to let you go?" His voice was rough, deeper than usual.

I wanted a lot of things. Distance between myself and Zyrus was at the bottom of that list.

I tilted my chin up and claimed his lips.

So much for self-defense.

16

ASTRID

ZYRUS WRAPPED his arms around me, one hand clutching the back of my head like he was afraid I might disappear if he didn't hold me tight to him. His mouth was hot against mine, lips firm and demanding in a way that made my knees weak.

I never wanted it to end.

His fingers tangled in my hair, and he held me impossibly closer. Everywhere we touched was a spark, a fire that threatened to consume me, but I didn't want to be free of it.

His tongue stroked mine, teasing me with a promise of so much more. I'd never been kissed like this, never been *wanted* like this. Except by him.

He pulled back, his eyes burning red and intense, and I wanted to chase the kiss, even as my senses tried to return. This wasn't moving slow. This wasn't taking our time. What if I hurt him again?

His fingers were still tangled in my hair, and I ached with the thought of losing his touch. But I shouldn't keep going, not knowing what might happen. "We should stop," I whispered, even as I tilted my head up to kiss him again.

His kiss was hot, scorching. My body molded to his, and I wanted to lose myself in him, but I couldn't. "Trust me, denya." His words were a rumble against my lips.

I trusted him more than anyone else. Even after such a short time. Or a long time apart. It was too hard to keep track of it when he was pressed up against me.

He trailed his fingers down my back, sending shivers up my spine. "If you want me to stop, pull away."

A simple request.

An impossible task.

He kissed me again, harder this time, his teeth grazing my lip. And I moaned. I couldn't help it.

He growled, a primal sound that sent my heart racing. My core pulsed with desire, a need I'd never felt for anyone else. Not like this.

He picked me up as if I weighed nothing and

carried me over to the couch. My head spun, but I didn't want him to stop, even if a small part of me thought we should.

He seemed fine. More than fine even.

He'd seemed fine the last time too.

But he set me down gently and then dropped to his knees in front of me, his eyes never leaving mine. I opened my mouth to tell him to stop, that he needed to be careful. But the look in his eyes froze my tongue.

This man, this alien, wanted to devour me.

And I was going to let him.

Whatever resistance there was, it left me then. I didn't know how to handle this thing between us, this bond I'd never known was possible. But our bodies understood one another.

"I want to see you," Zyrus growled. "All of you." His finger teased the edge of my shirt, and I followed the silent command, pulling it over my head and shimmying out of my pants until I was sitting naked on the couch in front of my mate.

My mate.

I really liked the sound of that.

His fingers danced over my skin, trailing heat in their wake. I could feel his gaze rake over me, studying me with an intensity that made me shiver. "You're beautiful," he murmured, his tone reverent.

I flushed under the praise, my skin tingling and my stomach fluttering. If he could do that to me with his words, his lips would destroy me.

And he was determined to try.

Zyrus leaned forward and kissed my thighs. It was the lightest brush of his mouth, barely there, but it was enough to send a jolt of pure pleasure through me. My legs fell open, giving him the access we both craved.

He shifted me so I was perched on the edge of the cushion, and then his head ducked down, his tongue sliding over me until he found my center. He teased and tortured me, making me writhe where I was, fingers digging into the fabric of the couch, hips arching up with every stroke of his tongue.

And then the monster pulled back, kissing my thighs and abdomen and everywhere *not* my sex until my body started to recover just enough to bring me down from that edge I was approaching.

That wasn't what I wanted.

I clutched his shoulders, desperate for something to hold on to, to anchor me. But he kept kissing me, driving me wild until I was clawing at him, my nails scraping his skin.

And then he licked me again, a long stroke that had me gasping out his name. He kept going, his tongue probing deep, exploring me with a focus that drove me crazy.

My body coiled tight, tension building until I felt like I was going to break.

And then I did.

A wave of pleasure rolled over me, my body arching off the couch, my sex pressing into his face, my fingers digging into his shoulders.

He stayed with me through every moment of it, holding me tight and bringing me through the orgasm until I collapsed, boneless, beneath him.

Zyrus lifted his head and grinned at me. "That's just the beginning," he said. His thick, hard cock was outlined in his pants, a temptation even as I lay there sated. "Let me have you, denya." He laid kisses along my stomach and up my neck until he finally found my lips.

The taste of myself on his mouth made me moan, and I wrapped my arms around his neck. I could feel his cock grinding against me, tempting me through that little bit of fabric.

Then he freed himself from his pants, and there was no barrier between us.

Just skin against skin.

Zyrus took himself in hand and rubbed the tip of his cock against my sex. The wetness there let him slide in easily.

And then he was pushing into me.

There was a moment of pressure as my body adjusted to the intrusion, stretching to accommodate him. It was a sweet ache, one I relished.

Then he pulled back and thrust again, the movement deep and hard and everything I craved.

He kissed me, his mouth slanting over mine as he filled me, his rhythm steady and measured. But I wanted more. Needed more.

"Faster," I begged.

And then he showed me exactly what a trained warrior could do.

He fucked me with a pace I could barely follow, his cock pounding into me and hitting that spot deep inside that made my vision go hazy.

He dipped his head and sucked on my nipple, his tongue hot and wet, his teeth sharp as they grazed my skin. It was more stimulation than I could handle, and yet I needed more.

It was perfect.

"More," I whimpered. "I need more."

Zyrus gave me everything I demanded. He

pushed me higher and higher, his mouth and hands on me, his cock inside me. I couldn't breathe.

And then he pulled back just a bit, his hips slowing ever so slightly.

But he didn't stop.

He didn't let up.

He found my hands and threaded our fingers together, holding me in place while he took me with a gentleness I hadn't thought him capable of.

It was that unexpected tenderness that finally tipped me over the edge again.

I came with a gasp, my body arching up off the couch and into his. He followed me over, his body stiffening, his cock twitching inside of me.

For a moment, all I could do was breathe.

My muscles relaxed, my heart slowing down. I clung to Zyrus and counted his breaths, remembered the awful moment last night when he collapsed.

He held on just as tight, and I let myself hope that this time things could be different.

17
ZYRUS

My mate was sated and sleeping, her chest rising and falling in a peaceful rhythm. I watched her for several moments, memorizing the curve of her cheek and the way her eyelashes fluttered against her skin. Reluctantly, I slid out of bed, wincing as the mattress creaked slightly. I pulled on my clothes quickly but quietly, not wanting to disturb her rest. The urge to crawl back into bed and watch her sleep for hours, maybe even days, was almost overwhelming. Her presence calmed something deep within me.

But there was something I had to do, had to know. A nagging thought that wouldn't let me rest, even in this moment of contentment. It pulled at me, demanding action despite my desire to stay.

My body thrummed with renewed energy, every muscle primed and ready for action. There was no trace of the debilitating weakness that had over-whelmed me after our first kiss and coupling. That was a good sign, and I dared to hope—still an unfa-miliar sensation—that it would last.

But hope wasn't enough. I needed certainty, cold hard facts to confirm what my instincts were telling me. The urgency of my mission pushed against the lingering warmth of our connection, demanding that I act now. I clenched my fists, steeling myself for what lay ahead. I needed to be absolutely sure.

It was only when I stood outside of Drex's door that I realized it was late. No one roamed the halls, and the lights were low to help simulate nighttime. Drex was likely sleeping beside his own mate; he wouldn't want to be disturbed. My questions could wait until morning.

But the door opened, and Drex stood there, his eyes alert despite the late hour. "I saw you on the view screen. Has something happened?" His voice was low, tinged with concern.

"Yes," I replied, suddenly aware of how much had transpired since we'd last spoken. I realized I hadn't told him about Yoree or my trip to the trash compactor. The weight of that information pressed on me. Drex wasn't my commanding officer, but it wasn't wise to keep such crucial details to myself. "May I come in?" I asked, glancing down the empty corridor.

He stepped aside to let me pass, his body tense. The room beyond was dimly lit, shadows clinging to the corners. "Is Astrid well?" Drex asked as soon as the door closed behind us, his worry evident in the tight set of his jaw.

"Yes, she's sleeping." Naked and satisfied. Mine.

There was an entertainment tablet on the low table and a blanket haphazardly piled to one side, as if hastily pushed away. Drex sat beside it, his posture suggesting he'd been there for quite some time. The faint glow from the tablet cast shadows across his face, accentuating the lines of fatigue around his eyes.

"This is a strange hour to be awake," I observed.

"I could say the same for you," Drex retorted, his tone equally hushed but tinged with a hint of dry humor. He picked up the tablet, his fingers moving with practiced ease as he flicked his hand to project the screen into the air between us. A message materialized, hovering in the dim light. It looked like some kind of shipping notification, the text crisp and official against the holographic background.

"This showed up just before I was going to go to bed," he explained, his eyes never leaving the projected image.

I leaned in closer, squinting to make out the details of the holographic message. Parts of it appeared to be handwritten, a strange mix of digital precision and personal touch that caught my attention.

"Did you order something from ..." I hesitated, deciphering the scrawled text. The characters seemed to dance in the dim light, challenging my vision. "... Honora Station?"

Drex's face tightened, a flicker of something—concern? anticipation? —passing over his features. "I did not."

With a practiced flick of his fingers, the image before us changed. Another message materialized, then vanished just as quickly. My eyes darted to keep up as he cycled through them rapidly, each one similar yet distinct.

"I've received five similar messages since I arrived on Nebula Outpost," Drex explained, his voice low and tinged with a hint of urgency that matched the tension I felt building in my own chest. "All of them roughly a week before a new soulless outcast showed up in a shipping container with a story of escaping an execution."

The implications of his words hit me like a physical blow. My mind raced, connecting dots I hadn't even realized existed. I clenched my fists, feeling the weight of this new information settle over me like a heavy cloak.

"Someone knows we're here." Of course someone knew we were here. How else would we have ended up together, a ragtag group of outcasts? My muscles tensed, readying for a fight that wasn't coming. "Do you think we're in danger?" I asked, my voice barely above a whisper, as if speaking too loudly might summon whatever threat loomed on the horizon.

Drex's eyes met mine, steady and calm despite the gravity of the situation. "Not from the Legion," he said, his tone reassuring but tinged with a hint of something else—anticipation, perhaps. "I think we're about to get a new soldier. They're in for a surprise." His gaze flicked towards the closed door to the bedroom where his denya was sleeping, a ghost of a smile playing at the corners of his mouth. I could almost feel the protective energy radiating from him, a fierce determination that matched my own growing resolve.

"It's been some time since anyone has joined us. Not since Jorin two years ago."

"Do you think something's changed in the Legion?" The Legion was a being of survival, the last vestige of a people that had been destroyed by an unknown enemy. Survival required change, but how much could the Legion change and still remain fundamentally Detyen?

"Something's changed with you," Drex said with a grin, his eyes glinting with a knowing look that made me shift uncomfortably. "Does it have something to do with the woman sleeping down the hall?"

My lip twitched, and I didn't understand why at first. A foreign sensation rippled through me, unfamiliar yet not unpleasant. And then I realized it was a smile. The muscles in my face felt unused, almost rusty. I cleared my throat, trying to regain my composure. "Astrid has some concerns about how I've reacted when we ... touch," I admitted, my voice low and hesitant.

Drex's eyebrows shot up, his expression a mix of surprise and amusement. "You passed out after a kiss?" he asked, leaning in closer as if we were sharing some great secret. The air between us seemed to crackle with an energy I couldn't quite name.

I felt heat rising to my cheeks, another unfamiliar sensation that left me feeling exposed. My hands clenched at my sides, seeking some form of control over these new, overwhelming feelings.

"Not just a kiss." Though I didn't want to go into minute details if it wasn't necessary.

"Congratulations to you, then. None of us know why it happens or what's happening, not really. But the same thing happened to me and to Ryklin. And ever since we completed the bond with our mates, we've been whole. No other symptoms. I don't think you have anything else to fear."

It was what I wanted to hear.

Now to convince my mate.

18
ASTRID

ZYRUS WAS WORKING another shift when the message buzzed on my communicator. The picture that came through almost made me throw the device across the room.

Alice. Tied up. Bruised. Her vibrant face marred with dark splotches and fear.

And a message: Sector J. Level nine. Come alone.

The words burned into my retinas, a sinister demand.

If Zyrus were with me, I would have said something. But alone, raw panic surged through me like an electric current. I threw on the first clothes I could grab, not caring if they matched or were even clean. My hands shook as I fumbled with the fastenings, and I ran out the door without pausing to plan or even catch my breath. The corridors of Nebula Outpost blurred around me as I sprinted.

Alice was hurt, and probably because of me. The guilt gnawed at my insides. I should have insisted that someone watch her, that if one of us was in danger, we both were. Now, as I raced towards an unknown threat, I cursed my own shortsightedness. The weight of responsibility pressed down on me, spurring me forward even as fear threatened to paralyze me.

Was this Yoree's doing? Mercy had been the only option I could stomach at the time; now I worried that I had sacrificed Alice to save that worthless piece of garbage.

I was halfway there when I realized I hadn't left any sort of message for Zyrus. My heart stuttered as the realization hit me. It was one thing to run off into danger alone, but it was beyond stupid not to leave a lifeline asking for backup. The cold metal walls of the station seemed to close in on me as I pushed forward, my breath coming in short gasps. I could have asked any of the other Detyens or their mates for help, but my feet carried me farther and farther away from where we all lived, the familiar corridors giving way to less traveled areas.

There hadn't been a time limit on that message,

but the implication had been clear enough. The longer I waited, the more Alice would pay for it. The thought made my stomach churn with dread. I could almost hear a clock ticking in my head, each second another potential moment of pain for Alice. The weight of my decision pressed down on me, making each step feel heavier than the last. But I couldn't turn back now, not when Alice's life hung in the balance.

I darted around people going about their daily lives with no idea my friend was being held hostage on the ship. I even nearly bowled over a woman in a station security uniform, and only managed to swerve around her at the last moment with a muttered apology.

Who had Alice? Why? And did this have anything to do with why my people were still stuck down on Nebula?

The thoughts were all a jumble in my head, none of them clear enough for me to follow the thread, especially not while I made for Sector J, level nine at a dead sprint. My lungs burned with each gasping breath, and the pounding of my feet on the metal floor echoed in my ears. Everything blurred together, each turn bringing me closer to an unknown threat and, hopefully, to Alice.

As I ran, my senses were on high alert. The acrid smell of industrial cleaner stung my nostrils, and the harsh fluorescent lights cast eerie shadows that seemed to dance at the edges of my vision. My muscles screamed in protest, but I pushed on, driven by a mixture of fear and determination. Time was slipping away, and with each passing moment, the danger to Alice—and possibly to my people on Nebula—grew more imminent.

It was clear why this was the sector Alice's attacker had chosen the second I crossed into it. The place was deserted, plastic tarps covering some of the walls, dust all over the floor. Heavy construction was underway here, and it wasn't fit for anyone.

At first, I had no idea where to go. I was on level nine and in Sector J. Then I spotted the red spots on the floor in front of me, and the smudges in the dust. Drag marks.

I had a trail to follow.

I really should have told someone I was going down there. I didn't want to die.

The sound of heavy breathing echoed down the hallway, and I slowed. How was I supposed to approach this? I didn't have a blaster with me to go in ready to shoot everyone and take no prisoners. I couldn't even escape a simple hold without falling into bed with Zyrus. That wasn't going to work now.

I just had to face this and hope for the best.

I never should have come alone.

But any chance of turning around was quashed when a large man in a station security uniform appeared behind me, cutting off my exit. He grabbed onto my arm, hard enough to bruise, and tugged me forward.

Alice was in a heap in the middle of an atrium. Her chest rose and fell, but one of her eyes was nearly swollen shut, and her clothes were torn and blood-spattered. They'd had her for some time, and they'd used that time to make her pay.

Two other hulking men flanked her, wearing dark clothes, but not station security uniforms. I didn't know if they worked on the station or if they'd been brought in by the boss.

The boss was obviously the short guy wearing an expensive suit and standing off to the side, looking down at his communicator and scrolling through messages as if he hadn't ordered the brutalization of an innocent woman. The guard holding me cleared his throat, and the guy in the suit looked up.

"Thank you for joining us, Astrid. I was worried

you wouldn't make it." He slid his communicator into his pocket with a smooth, practiced motion. The device disappeared into the folds of his expensive suit, leaving no visible trace. "My name is Vastrien Roqhart."

The name hung in the air, heavy with unspoken significance. Fear was acrid on my tongue, but I forced myself to speak.

"Is that supposed to mean something?" I sneered, the words tumbling out before I could stop them. Instantly, I regretted my bravado. My eyes darted to Alice's crumpled form on the floor, and my stomach clenched with dread. She was *right there*, vulnerable and already battered. I knew with sickening certainty that she'd pay for my sins, for every careless word that left my mouth. The weight of my mistake pressed down on me, making it hard to breathe in the tense, oppressive atmosphere of the atrium.

But Vastrien smiled, and it sent a chill down my spine. "No, I suppose it's difficult to keep track of every assistant and junior executive when you're busy on the ground. I work for Intergalactic Minerals. Does that ring a bell? Or the Nebula Mining Conglomerate?"

Those were names I knew. Names me and everyone down on Nebula had cursed for a decade.

"Ah, yes, now you're getting it. You and this one here are trying to cause trouble for us." He nodded at the man who was still clutching my arm, his fingers digging painfully into my flesh. With a rough shove, I was propelled towards a nearby bench.

I stumbled, my heart racing as I fought to keep my balance. My hands caught the edge of the cold metal seat just in time, and I managed to right myself before I could topple over. The sudden movement sent a jolt of pain through my still-healing injuries. Anger bubbled up inside me, hot and fierce.

"Trouble?" I spat, my voice trembling with barely contained rage. "You assholes left us on Nebula to die! We survived for ten years in that hellhole because of you!"

One of the men in black took a threatening step towards Alice, his massive frame looming over her battered body. The sound of his heavy boots on the floor echoed ominously in the atrium. My stomach lurched, and I clamped my mouth shut, the taste of fear bitter on my tongue. The weight of my words hung in the air, and I silently prayed they wouldn't cost Alice any more pain.

"An unfortunate ... misunderstanding," Vastrien

said, searching for that last word for a moment. "We do not stand for insurrection."

"Insurrection? What?" Was he still talking about the mine? Or something else? "Are you saying the explosion was sabotage?" I'd rebuffed ten years of conspiracy theories from people with nothing better to do than think. And now this stranger was telling me they might have been right?

"Quarterly earnings reports suggest a lot of things, Astrid. And it's been a decade. People have forgotten about that unfortunate accident, and my superiors are not eager for people to remember. So, you see why I have a problem."

"I just want my people off Nebula. No one gives a shit about Intergalactic Minerals." Sure, we'd done our fair share of cursing the company while we were trapped, but now wasn't the time to mention that.

Vastrien pulled out his communicator and began reading off the screen. "Ideas to make Intergalactic Minerals get off their asses and do something. One: sue them. Two: find a reporter and get the story out. Three: release rats into their headquarters. Four: find even more reporters. Five ... shall I go on? Or do you understand now?"

"Understand what?" I really should have left a

note. Or waited for Zyrus. Or done anything except walk into this trap.

"This message was sent to you by Alice over there two days ago. You've been plotting to take us down. And in conjunction with both of your activities on this station, interfering with security and sending messages to media officials in the Oscavian Empire ..."

"What? I never even read that message! How did you get that? Are you monitoring our comms?" I vaguely remembered Alice sending me something, but I'd been caught up with Zyrus and everything else. Besides, I hadn't done that—or at least not all of it.

"Cadence Carper, a junior executive at a small Oscavian news network," Vastrien said, his voice dripping with disdain. "The messages may be encrypted, but we know Alice was in communication with her. Our intelligence is quite thorough."

On the ground, Alice made a sound of protest, a strangled mix of pain and defiance. Without warning, one of the brutes kicked her in the stomach, the sickening thud of his boot connecting with her flesh echoing through the atrium. I flinched, my own body tensing in sympathetic pain as Alice curled into herself, gasping for air.

"Get her out of here," Vastrien snarled, his face contorting with disgust. "I won't deal with both of them at once. It's too much of a headache." He waved his hand dismissively, as if Alice were nothing more than an annoying insect.

At his command, two of the brutes scooped Alice up, their meaty hands gripping her arms with bruising force. They dragged her away, her feet scraping against the floor as she weakly tried to resist. I watched helplessly as they disappeared around a corner, leaving just me, Vastrien, and the station security guard hovering over me. The sudden absence of Alice made the space feel colder, more threatening. I swallowed hard, my throat dry with fear, as I realized I was now alone with these men who seemed to hold my fate in their hands.

"All we want is to get our people safely off of Nebula. That's what I've been trying to do for weeks. And Alice wants off the station altogether. She has a family." But I didn't tell him that her wife was Cadence. What if that put the woman in more danger? My heart raced, the weight of Alice's secret pressing down on me like a physical force. I could almost taste the metallic tang of fear in my mouth as I struggled to keep my expression neutral.

"And all I want is to clean up this mess and

never see this sector again. I hope you understand, it's nothing personal." He nodded towards the station security guard behind me. The hairs on the back of my neck stood up as I heard the subtle shift of the guard's stance. My muscles tensed, ready to react, though I knew any attempt to flee would be futile. The air in the room seemed to thicken, making it harder to breathe as I waited for whatever was coming next.

I felt a prick in my arm, and everything went black.

19
ZYRUS

My chest pounded with every breath, and I couldn't pinpoint the reason. My skin felt too tight, as if something inside of me was ready to burst out at any moment. Sweat beaded on my forehead, and I could taste the metallic tang of fear in my mouth.

And then, abruptly, it went silent. The usual hum of life faded away, leaving an eerie stillness that set my nerves on edge.

There were still hours left in my shift, the clock on the wall ticking away relentlessly. But nothing could have kept me there, not with the bone-deep certainty that something was terribly wrong. My instincts screamed at me to move, to act.

Astrid. The thought of her was a beacon in my mind. I needed to get to my mate, and fast. My legs were already moving before I'd fully formed the thought, propelling me towards the exit with unstoppable urgency.

She was supposed to be in our room. She'd promised to stay there or to stick with one of the others. But every step that brought me closer felt like a step in the wrong direction.

The room was empty.

One look, and I knew. But I still looked further, into the bedroom and bathroom, even opening up the door to the closet as if she might have fallen into another dimension.

She wasn't there.

Rage and fear warred inside of me, a volatile mix that threatened to overwhelm my senses. Had someone *taken* her? The possibility made my blood boil at the thought. I scanned the room frantically, searching for any sign of a struggle, any clue that might hint at why my mate wasn't where she had promised she would be. But the space was unnervingly pristine, offering no answers to the questions that screamed in my mind.

My fists clenched at my sides, knuckles white with tension. I would tear the station apart to find her if I had to. Every corridor, every hidden nook, every airlock—nowhere was off-limits. The need to locate Astrid consumed me, driving out all other thoughts and concerns. Time was of the essence, and I couldn't shake the feeling that each passing second put her in greater danger.

Determination settled over my shoulders, calming the turbulent emotions enough for me to think. I forced myself to breathe. One deep inhale after the other. It was easy, automatic, and it helped me focus.

Where would Astrid go?

Surely she would have told the others.

I scanned the room one last time, half-expecting to find a hastily scrawled note from Astrid tucked away somewhere. But there was nothing. A pang of frustration mixed with worry shot through me. This thing between us was still new, raw, and uncertain in many ways. We were still learning each other's quirks and habits, the unspoken language of a newly bonded pair. I couldn't shake the nagging feeling that I should have known, should have sensed something was amiss sooner.

My jaw clenched as I marched out of the room, my footsteps heavy with purpose. I reached Drex's door in what felt like seconds, my fist already raised. I pounded on the metal surface with enough force to make my knuckles ache, the sound reverberating through the corridor. The noise echoed down the hallway in both directions, and I didn't care who heard, as long as Drex opened the stars-damned door.

I was one heartbeat away from ramming my shoulder into the door, consequences be damned, when it slid open with a soft hiss. My fist froze mid-air, poised for another thunderous knock that never came. The sudden lack of resistance nearly threw me off-balance, both physically and mentally. A small, detached part of my mind registered relief that I hadn't needed to resort to more drastic measures. But that relief was quickly swallowed by the pressing need to find Astrid, to know she was safe.

"Astrid's gone." I didn't recognize the ragged tone of my own voice. I'd spoken like the soulless for so long that any inflection was a stranger, let alone this desperation.

Then I noticed Ryklin and Noelle were sitting at the table with Pippa, all of them looking intently at a message on a holo-projector. Their faces were bathed in the soft blue glow, expressions tense and focused. The sight momentarily pulled me up short, a flicker of hope igniting in my chest. Maybe they knew something I didn't.

Drex pulled me farther inside, his grip firm but

not unkind. Slowing down felt like betraying my mate, every second wasted another moment Astrid could be in danger. I had to look like a madman—hair disheveled, eyes wild, chest heaving with barely contained panic. I wanted to turn around and run *somewhere*. Anywhere to find Astrid. The urge to move, to act, thrummed through my body like an electric current.

"What's going on?" Noelle asked, her brow furrowed with concern as she looked up from the holo-projector. Her gaze swept over me, taking in my disheveled state. "Where's Astrid?"

The question hung in the air, heavy and loaded. I swallowed hard, my throat suddenly dry. The room felt too small, too still, the recycled air of the station thick with tension. I could hear the faint hum of the life support systems, a sound I usually ignored but now seemed deafening in the expectant silence.

"I don't know." The words came out through gritted teeth and a clenched jaw. "She's not in her room. I felt—" I didn't know how to describe it and speaking of emotion felt like a crime. Not too long ago, it could have gotten me killed. It had already given me a death sentence once. But the men in this room understood exactly what I was going through. They wouldn't hold it against me.

I may have known that logically, but it meant nothing to the fist that had my heart in its grip. My chest felt tight, each breath a struggle against the weight of fear pressing down on me.

"Tell us," Drex said, his voice low and steady. He didn't make me move any farther, seeming to understand my need to stay poised for action. The others leaned in, their faces a mix of concern and anticipation.

"I felt ... something ... while I was working," I began, forcing the words out past the lump in my throat. "A burst of emotions and adrenaline. It hit me like a physical blow." I swallowed hard, remembering the intensity of the sensation. "Then it went quiet, eerily so. I knew I needed to see Astrid immediately." My hands clenched and unclenched at my sides as I continued. "I went to her room, and she's not there. No note, no sign of where she might have gone." There it was. Clinical, a report I could almost give a superior, except for the panic attack threatening to overtake me. My heart raced, and I could feel a cold sweat breaking out on my forehead. The air suddenly felt too thin, not enough to fill my lungs.

Ryklin was standing, and Drex bent down to pull on his boots.

"I want you and Pippa to search Astrid's room for anything Zyrus might have missed," Ryklin told his mate. She nodded.

Drex placed a hand on his chest, his expression softening with understanding. "You should be able to feel the bond between the two of you. It's like a homing beacon, a thread connecting your souls. Close your eyes and concentrate on that connection."

A part of me resisted, my jaw clenching as I fought against the suggestion. He wanted me to follow some buried, ancient instinct that had been torn out of me at the end of a scalpel and only barely begun to heal? The idea seemed absurd, almost cruel. My hands curled into fists at my sides, nails digging into my palms.

But beneath the resistance, a desperate hope flickered. If there was even the slightest chance this could lead me to Astrid, I had to try. I took a deep breath, the taste of filtered oxygen sharp on my tongue, and forced myself to relax. Slowly, reluctantly, I let my eyes drift closed.

Anything for my mate.

I closed my eyes and breathed deep, filling my lungs with the familiar metallic tang of station air. The panic was still there, a living thing clawing at my insides, fear threatening to choke me and pull me down to somewhere I'd never escape. My heart raced, pounding against my ribcage as if trying to break free. And below the fear was doubt, insidious and corrosive. Was I good enough for Astrid? Could I be the mate she needed, after everything I'd been through? What if I lost my soul again and she was stuck at the side of some emotionless automaton, a shell of the man she deserved?

I clenched my jaw, fighting against the tide of negative emotions. This wasn't helping. I had to focus. And then, as if responding to my determination, I sensed it—below the doubt was the faint glow of our bond. It was barely perceptible, a whisper of warmth in the cold void of my fear. But it was there. With a surge of desperate hope, I reached out with my mind, imagining my hands wrapping around that tenuous connection. I tugged, putting all my will behind the action, praying it would lead me to Astrid.

My eyes snapped open, and I rushed out the door.

20

ASTRID

WHATEVER HE GAVE me didn't knock me out for long. At least, I was pretty sure it didn't.

My head was pounding, and I tried to lift a hand to rub at it, but my arms were tied down beside me. It was dark. Or my vision was busted. I couldn't tell which. I squinted, and all I could make out was blinking lights in front of me.

"Hurry it up!" That was Vastrien's angry voice, but he sounded like he was screaming from the other side of the room.

"It's not designed to launch yet." I didn't recognize the other man. But whatever they were trying to do, I had to get out of there before they succeeded.

My vision gradually cleared, adjusting to the dim surroundings as the drug's effects wore off.

With each passing second, more details came into focus, and a sinking feeling grew in the pit of my stomach.

The blinking lights I'd noticed earlier formed a pattern now—instrument panels, switches, and gauges. There was no mistaking it. I was strapped into what looked like a cockpit, surrounded by unfamiliar controls and readouts. My mind raced, trying to make sense of the situation. Why would they put me there? I had zero experience piloting any kind of craft, let alone whatever this was.

Then it hit me. Vastrien wasn't giving me a chance to escape. No, this was far more sinister. He wanted me to crash. The realization sent a chill down my spine. He was setting me up, planning to make my death look like a tragic accident. I had to find a way out of this, and fast.

I didn't need him explaining the whole plan. It was pretty simple, actually. Stick me in a craft, tie me to the chair, and let nature take its course.

That barely counted as murder.

Zyrus.

I wanted him here so much it hurt, a deep ache in my chest that threatened to overwhelm me. Not just for the rescue, though that would be very much appreciated given my current predicament. No, I needed him by my side to give me strength, to anchor me in this moment of fear and uncertainty. His steady presence would have been a lifeline, helping me focus and find a way out of this mess. But he wasn't there, and I had to face this alone. I clenched my jaw, pushing down the longing and forcing myself to concentrate on the task at hand. Escape first, reunite later.

Ugh. I never would have been in this mess if I had just waited for him. Or left a note. Or done literally anything but run straight for danger like an idiot.

Was Alice still alive?

She had to be. If not, all of this was for nothing, and I was about to die and never get to know what life would be like with my mate. All that fear, all that hesitation, it was gone now.

If Zyrus were here right now, I'd kiss him and never let him go.

But he wasn't. And Vastrien and the other guy were bickering too quietly for me to hear.

I didn't think they knew I was awake yet. Their hushed voices still carried on, oblivious to my growing awareness. That gave me a small advantage, but for how long?

I struggled against my bonds some more,

twisting my wrists, searching for any give. The straps bit into my skin, unyielding. Whoever had tied me up knew what they were doing. These weren't amateur knots; they were expertly crafted to keep me firmly in place.

Where was I exactly? The air felt stale and carried a faint metallic scent.

It was too quiet to be the normal transport depot. Even in the middle of the night that place was bustling with ships coming and going. Time was a polite fiction on a space station, especially from ships coming from hundreds of light years away.

This had to be a repair port, one for smaller craft.

The one in Sector J.

That was where they'd lured me. The repair port in Sector J, currently undergoing maintenance. No one would think to search there, its isolation making it the perfect spot for Vastrien's scheme. The realization sank in my gut like a stone.

My situation was dire. Even if I managed to break free from these restraints, I'd need to sprint across the entire sector before finding anyone who could assist. The vast, empty corridors stretched out in my mind, a daunting obstacle course. And I had no clue how many of the station's crew were in

Vastrien's pocket. For all I knew, every face I encountered could be an enemy, ready to drag me back to this death trap. The odds were stacked against me.

I had to put that worry aside. All that mattered right now was getting out of the ship before they launched it.

There was a small light blinking on the dash, and I read the warning.

Low oxygen.

Damn it. Vastrien wasn't taking any chances. Even if I managed to get free and somehow get this thing under control, I'd only have the air I was currently breathing, and once that ran out, I'd be dead.

I became acutely aware of every breath, the rise and fall of my chest suddenly loud in my ears. I tried to keep them shallow and spaced, counting the seconds between each inhale. But the more I focused on it, the deeper I breathed, my lungs desperate for the air they were sure they were about to lose. The metallic taste of fear coated my tongue as I fought against the urge to gulp down oxygen. My heart raced, pumping blood that seemed to roar through my veins, each beat a reminder of how precious little time I had left. The edges of my vision started to blur. I clenched my fists, nails digging into my palms, using the sharp sting to anchor myself and resist the temptation to hyperventilate.

Stop it.

I'd been through worse. I'd survived an explosion that had killed hundreds of my friends and co-workers. I'd spent a decade eking out existence on a planet with few supplies and no knowledge of rough living. I didn't shrink away from hard situations.

And I knew how to handle freaking knots.

Rope, that was something we had plenty of down on Nebula. Not only the stuff that had survived the mine explosion, but we'd managed to learn how to weave it out of the vines and fibers available to us on land. I wasn't going to let a bit of rope be my downfall.

I tested the bonds again. And there was give on my left side. Not enough to wriggle out, but it was a start. I worked my wrist back and forth, ignoring the way it burned against my skin. I'd be red and raw by the time I was out of this, but I'd be free.

That was all that mattered.

Outside the craft, I heard the metallic clank of gears turning, and my head snapped forward. Massive bay doors loomed before me, their imposing presence a stark reminder of my precarious situation. Those doors would lead to the airlock, the final barrier between me and the cold void of space where they planned to launch my ship into oblivion. The sound of machinery echoed through the chamber, each grinding noise a countdown to my potential demise. I gritted my teeth, redoubling my efforts to free myself. The rough texture of the rope bit into my skin as I twisted and pulled, but I ignored the pain. My eyes darted around the cockpit, searching for anything that might aid my escape. Time was running out, and I could almost feel the vacuum of space reaching for me through those unyielding doors.

The clanking stopped, and more cursing came from where Vastrien and his lackey were working.

I was running out of time.

I yanked my arm as hard as I could, biting my lip until I tasted blood. It felt like I was going to pull my thumb off, but then with a *pop*, my hand came free.

It hurt so much I wanted to cry. The last thing I wanted to do was use my aching hand to undo the knot holding my other arm in place. My fingers felt like sausages, and I wanted to plunge them in an ice bath for the next several days.

There was no time for complaint.

The metal started to clang again, and the bay doors in front of me opened inch by inch.

My ship was probably on a conveyor of some kind. I had no way to stop it. I just had to get out.

I worked the knot with quickly numbing fingers, slippery with blood. I dug in, desperate to loosen the knot, and it felt like no matter what I did, it wouldn't work.

Until the knot went slack, and the ropes dropped to the floor.

I opened the door to the cockpit just a crack and slid out, careful on the steps, hoping I wasn't making any noise. The rest of the craft must have been between me and wherever Vastrien and his minion were, and I said a little prayer of thanks to anyone who was listening.

I was carefully climbing down a ladder off the ship, but before I could step off, I noticed the drop.

It was open under me, an entire maintenance bay that went down two or three stories, a sheer drop I'd be lucky to survive.

The clanging of the bay doors stopped.

And then the craft began to move.

21

ZYRUS

RYKLIN CURSED when we entered Sector J, but none of us slowed down. The bond between Astrid and I was growing stronger with every step, and I knew we must be getting closer. We'd run out of station soon enough if we weren't.

What if she'd been taken off the station?

I'd lost her once, I refused to lose her again.

There was a loud metal-on-metal screech coming from farther down the corridor, and I sped up, putting everything I had into the final sprint.

A door labeled SHIP REPAIR, SECTOR J slid open when we came into range. There were two men in the room, both human, one wearing a black jumpsuit and the other dressed for the boardroom.

"You can't be in here," the well-dressed man sputtered.

Instinct had me punching him in the face before sense could catch up. He crumpled, and the other man pulled a blaster.

But Drex was quicker. He lunged and caught the man's wrist, twisting it until the weapon fell to the floor. Drex drove his elbow into the man's face, and he went down, right next to his boss.

Where was Astrid?

The screeching of the door opening stopped but was followed by a blaring horn and the sound of a metal conveyor belt starting up.

We were in a small control room with a large window that looked out into the repair bay where a severely damaged ship was slowly being pushed towards the open bay doors that led to the air lock.

And the bond inside me screamed that Astrid was there.

I moved without thought, even when Ryklin grabbed hold of my shirt to keep me from sprinting into danger. We didn't know if there were more hostiles out there. All I knew was that Astrid needed me.

On the ground, the men were starting to groan

and come to, but Drex had grabbed the fallen blaster and had it trained on both of them.

"Let him go," he told Ryklin.

The hold on me vanished.

I went through the door into the repair bay, calling Astrid's name. A part of me expected an assault of blaster fire or worse, but there was nothing.

Until there was a feminine scream.

I ran towards the slowly moving ship and nearly plunged into the repair bay under the thin conveyor belt that was holding it up. But it was the sight of Astrid hanging from the ladder on the opposite side that stopped me cold.

She was dangling from the edge, her body trembling, fingertips white with the effort of holding on and slipping by the second. She looked up, and her eyes went wide.

"Zyrus! I can't hold on." Her fingers spasmed, and her shoulders jerked, but she didn't fall.

It was like an explosion went off inside of me. Adrenaline flooded through me, and I didn't hesitate. I leapt forward and ran down the center of the conveyor belt, the sound of the grinding machinery and the scraping of the ship's hull on the ground thundering in my ears.

I wouldn't let Astrid fall.

I finally closed the distance between us and grasped her hand, jerking her up onto the conveyor under the ship. We were nearly through the air lock doors, and Astrid was breathing hard. I wanted to clutch her close and kiss her until we both forgot how to breathe.

Later.

I kept a tight hold on her wrist and carefully guided her under the drooping wing of the broken ship. But the conveyor was still moving us forward, and now that I was paying attention, it was faster than I thought. We moved forward, but it still pulled us back. And with the miniscule width, we had to be careful about how we stepped. One wrong move, and we'd plunge at least ten meters and two stories below.

Why hadn't Ryklin or Drex stopped the conveyor belt?

We were too far into the air lock to see what they were doing, and I couldn't waste time worrying about that, not when my mate and I needed to get out of there.

"When those doors close, the exterior door is going to open," Astrid yelled over the clanking around us. "We need to get out of here."

"Trying!" The ship was no hope. One wing drooped lifelessly to the side, and I could see a gigantic crack in the hull. We might last a few extra minutes with the ambient oxygen in the craft, but it was even worse than a last resort, and I wasn't about to try it. "I need you to trust me."

She put her hand in mine. "I do."

I swung Astrid onto my back and let my instincts drive me, one gigantic step after another clearing the conveyor belt until I was past the bay doors and we were out of some of the danger.

Until a wide blaster shot nearly had me and Astrid toppling down the drop. With no ship to dodge, it was easier to keep my balance, but with my mate clinging to me, my center of gravity was off, and I almost fell anyway.

We came to a walkway, and I stepped onto solid ground, carefully letting my mate back down to her feet. Then my claws were out, and I was ready to fight.

But Ryklin and Drex had it under control. The man in the suit was in a different position now, jacket smoking from where a blaster shot had hit him in the shoulder, knocking him out. The other man had his hands raised and wasn't trying to fight.

"He had a hidden blaster," said Drex.

That explained the stray shot.

"Is Alice here?" Astrid looked around my shoulder, eyes darting around the cavernous room. "They have Alice. We have to find her."

I cursed. Of course they had Alice. Putting someone else in peril was the only reason my mate would have run off like she did. And judging by how we'd found Astrid, I feared for Alice's chances. And, unlike with Astrid, we had no hope of tracking her.

Drex was tying up the two men when I crouched down in front of the man who was still conscious. "Where's the other woman?"

"I don't know!" He jerked his shoulders, like he was trying to wave his hands around.

"Astrid ..." She didn't need to see this.

"If you're going to torture him, I'm not stepping out of the room. Not this time. Where's Alice?" She took a menacing step forward.

The man looked between all four of us and came to the right decision. "I really don't know for sure. But we've been using a couple of rooms in this sector." He listed them.

I nodded to Drex, and he shot the man, using the lowest setting on the blaster. It would knock him out for awhile but no other harm done.

It would have been faster to split up, but we

didn't know how many people were holding Alice or if more of Vastrien's men were skulking around Sector J. The first room was empty, but there was evidence that someone had been using it—disturbed dust and boxes set up as chairs.

We heard the shouting before we made it to the second room.

"Put it down, Yoree!" That wasn't Alice's voice.

Drex, Ryklin, and I set up a formation, Astrid hanging back without being told. We approached the door, Drex in front since he was the only one with a blaster.

Two shots rang out, and they didn't come from him.

There was more commotion, and we bust through the door to find a woman kneeling beside Alice's chair and working at her bonds, with Yoree and another man unconscious on the floor. She jerked her blaster up when she heard us enter.

It was the woman who'd been following Astrid and Pippa a few weeks ago. She was wearing her station security uniform.

She lowered the blaster. "Everything is under control," she said. "I'm with security. This is a restricted area, and you need to clear out."

"Give me the blaster, Drex." I held out my hand,

and he placed it in my palm. It felt like an old friend as I pointed it at the woman. "You're working for them."

The woman's brow furrowed in confusion, but her blaster didn't falter.

On the chair, Alice moaned in pain, barely conscious.

The woman gritted her teeth. "Yoree there paid me two hundred credits to follow some woman around for a few days. Then I got suspicious when that bastard showed up with a black eye and offered me more to do worse. I've been tracking him ever since. And as soon as I get this woman to medical, I'm arresting everyone in Sector J, and I'll let a judge sort it out on a penal colony a million miles from here."

Could I believe her?

She lowered her blaster and started working on Alice's bonds again, heedless of the weapon I had trained on her.

"There are two more men over by the repair bay." Astrid slipped in behind us. She came up next to me and put her hand on my arm, guiding the blaster down. "They've been trying to make sure that no one can get off of Nebula. I have a hundred people down there waiting for a rescue."

The security woman cursed. "One more freaking mess." The rope came free, and Alice slumped to her side as if strings holding her up had been cut. "Give me two days, and if they're not up here ... "

We waited for her to finish.

Astrid walked forward and helped Alice up. She was conscious enough to stand, but barely. "I'll hold you to that," said my mate.

And we left the scene.

22

ASTRID

ALICE WAS GOING to be okay. The med team was very confident, and Zyrus had asked two of his fellow Detyens—Kaelor and Jorin—to hold vigil outside her door to make sure nothing bad happened to her. She'd woken up long enough to tell me she was ready to get the hell off this station.

And I was waiting for the other shoe to drop.

I carefully flexed my fingers and toes, wincing at the dull ache that radiated through my body. Apart from a smattering of bruises and a few tender spots, I'd somehow escaped relatively unscathed. The silence from Zyrus, however, was deafening. He hadn't uttered a single word about my ill-fated encounter with Vastrien, but I could sense the tension rolling off him in waves. His jaw was clenched, his eyes a swirling storm of crimson.

I'd royally screwed up. Sneaking away without a word, recklessly throwing myself into danger's path —I might as well have painted a target on my back. By all rights, I should be dead. The gravity of my actions hit me like a punch to the gut.

So why wasn't Zyrus tearing into me? His eerie calm unnerved me more than any shouting match ever could. I swallowed hard, the taste of fear bitter on my tongue as I waited for the inevitable explosion.

"I'm sorry," I said as I crawled into bed beside him. "I shouldn't have run off like that. I saw the message, and I panicked." And Alice had been the one to ultimately pay the price for all of it. I'd spent the last few weeks certain they'd come for me and left her undefended.

"I'm not angry." Zyrus pulled his shirt over his head and let it fall to the floor. It made concentrating on what we were talking about a bit difficult. "It should be over now. We're finally together. I'm not going to waste any more time on getting upset over the past." He noticed that my eyes hadn't moved from his chest. "Were you going to continue this heartfelt apology, or ..." He let his fingers trail over the muscles of his abs.

I liked "or."

I clambered to my knees, the cool sheets sliding off my skin as I made my way across the bed. The mattress dipped and shifted beneath me with each awkward movement, but I didn't care. My focus was solely on Zyrus. Heart pounding, I reached out and grasped his shoulders, feeling the warmth of his skin beneath my palms. Without hesitation, I tugged him towards me and pressed my lips against his, savoring the electric spark that jolted through my body at the contact. The taste of him, familiar yet thrilling, made my head spin as I deepened the kiss, desperate to convey everything I couldn't put into words.

I melted into Zyrus, his lips grazing mine with an electrifying tenderness that quickly ignited into fierce passion. His mouth seared against my own, demanding and unyielding, as his powerful arms encircled me. He pulled me flush against his chest, eliminating any space between us until I was engulfed by his presence. My fingertips glided over the planes of his torso, marveling at the contrast between his impossibly smooth skin and the rock-hard muscles beneath. Every inch of him radiated heat, setting my nerves ablaze as I lost myself in his embrace. The scent of him—a heady mix of spice and something uniquely alien—filled my senses, drowning out everything else until there was nothing left in my world but Zyrus.

I savored every moment of contact with Zyrus, relishing the feel of his skin beneath my fingertips and the taste of his lips on mine. The steady thrum of his heart against my chest sent shivers down my spine, a constant reminder that this was real, that he was there with me. The intensity of our connection left me dizzy, overwhelmed by emotions I'd never dared to hope for. As we clung to each other, the gravity of my recent actions hit me anew. I'd nearly lost all of this—lost him—because of one stupid, bravado-filled charge. The thought made my stomach clench, but I pushed it aside, determined to focus on the present and the man in my arms.

I gasped and had to pull away.

Zyrus cupped my cheek, his eyes glowing red with emotion. "We're here now. It's okay."

I kissed him again.

I never wanted to stop kissing him, not for the rest of my life. I craved the sensation of his tongue exploring my mouth, his strong hands gripping my hips, our breaths mingling in a heated exchange.

Every fiber of my being yearned to belong to him completely, to claim him as mine in return. The intensity of my desire almost overwhelmed me, but I couldn't get enough.

Reluctantly, I broke away from his lips, immediately missing their warmth. My heart raced as I trailed kisses down the sharp line of his jaw, savoring the slight roughness against my lips. I made my way to his neck, inhaling his intoxicating scent. There was something else I'd been fantasizing about for a while, an urge I could no longer ignore. My pulse quickened as I prepared to act on this long-held desire.

I made my way down his body, my hand landing over the band holding up the sleep pants his was wearing. "Let's get rid of these."

He didn't need more convincing. And then he laid back in all his glory. Naked and hard and totally mine. I licked my lips in anticipation. I couldn't wait to taste him.

But instead of getting right down to him, I trailed kisses across his hips and thighs. Teasing, tasting, enjoying him in a way I'd fantasized about for weeks.

He growled with frustration under me, his fists clenching and unclenching like he was trying to stop himself from grabbing my head and taking control. I hummed with appreciation at that show of restraint and sank my mouth down around his cock until I nearly choked, then rose up and began a slow, tortuous rhythm, learning every ridge and curve until I knew him by heart.

His next growl was deep and hungry, and it made me tremble with need, but I didn't stop. Not a chance. Not when I could turn him on so completely, when his iron self-control was melting away and leaving only pleasure behind.

I wanted to savor this forever, this powerful feeling of controlling my mate's pleasure, of giving him everything he needed while he gasped and jerked beneath me.

But he could only take so much, and when I pulled back, he stopped me from diving in again, a wicked grin on his face.

"My turn."

And whether or not I wanted to stop savoring him, Zyrus was in control. He rocked me back on the bed, my clothes disappearing in a skilled flick of his claws until I was naked, my legs splayed wide, and he was between them, tongue deep inside of me.

I bucked my hips with abandon, lost in the sensations he gave me. He worked me with his fingers and his mouth, driving me higher and higher until I lost all sense of everything but him. Until the only thing in my universe was pleasure and him.

When he sank into me, his cock filling me to the brim, my breath left my lungs in a long exhale, and I clung to him with everything I had. He started out with gentle thrusts, letting the pleasure build slowly and deliberately. I reached up and clutched at his shoulders, encouraging him to give me more.

And when he did, it was like a dam breaking inside of me. The heat rushed through me, flooding my veins and sparking along my nerves. Every inch of my body ached with it, and I never wanted it to end.

My body trembled with ecstasy, and he held me in place, keeping us close so that nothing could interrupt this moment. This perfect joining where we were becoming one.

I was on the verge of bursting, and I let go, coming harder than I ever had in my life, clinging to Zyrus as he joined me in tumbling over that edge.

We couldn't stop touching each other, not even when our bodies untangled and the sweat began to cool. He had an arm wrapped around my shoulders, and I kept tracing the clan markings on his chest.

"The second I saw you on this station, I knew

there was something there." I leaned in and brushed my lips against his chest, savoring the warmth of his skin. "I'm sorry I didn't realize it sooner. That we had to wait so long. All that time wasted when we could have been together."

"We're together now, denya. And I'm not letting you go." Zyrus's arms tightened around me, his voice a low rumble that vibrated through his chest. I pressed closer, breathing in his scent and savored the steady thrum of his heartbeat against my cheek.

23
ZYRUS

LEAVING my mate asleep in our bed was getting more difficult by the day. I would have expected it to become easier, a task improved by practice. But whenever I saw her lying there, all I wanted to do was wake her up, give her the pleasure she deserved, and remind her that she was mine.

The sight of her peaceful form, nestled in the sheets, tugged at something primal within me. Her scent lingered in the air, a constant reminder of our bond. I found myself pausing longer each morning, torn between duty and desire. My fingers itched to trace the curve of her shoulder, to feel the warmth of her skin. It took every ounce of willpower to turn away and face the day, knowing that my denya would be waiting for me when I returned.

All I wanted was her.

Instead, I was sitting in Ryklin's quarters with Drex and the other soulless Detyens, all of us contemplating the message Drex had displayed on the holo-projector.

"You never mentioned these messages before," said Kaelor. He and Jorin were no longer watching Alice. She'd woken up after two days in the medbay and insisted on getting on the first flight off Nebula Outpost. By now, she had to be halfway to the Oscavian Empire.

"The situation has changed." Drex nodded to Ryklin and me. The tension in the room thickened, pressing against my skin like an invisible weight.

"Because you've recovered your emotions," Jorin said, his voice flat. He leaned forward, elbows on his knees, scrutinizing Drex. "Why does that concern you? Isn't that what you wanted?"

It was unsettling to hear Thalor, Jorin, and Kaelor speak now. The absence of inflection, of vitality, in their voices was stark and unmistakable. The flatness grated on my nerves, a constant reminder of what they'd lost. Until a couple of weeks ago, I hadn't noticed it.

Now, the contrast between their monotone and

the rich emotions in my own voice was jarring. I found myself straining to detect even the slightest hint of feeling in their words, but there was nothing. Just empty shells of the Detyens they once were, their voices as lifeless as the cold metal walls surrounding us.

"It goes beyond anything we've ever heard of the soulless doing. And it may put all of us at risk." Ryklin paused for a moment before continuing. "I wonder if we should try contacting someone, letting them know what we've discovered—that the denya bond can heal the soulless."

I felt my own bond with Astrid pulse in my chest.

"If we've figured it out, surely they can," Drex said, his voice tinged with concern. "There are six of us and thousands of them."

"Do you think they know?" I asked, a chill running down my spine. It had been so long since I'd thought of the Legion, their presence a distant memory faded by time.

I hadn't bothered to wonder if they'd changed in the years since I'd arrived on Nebula Outpost. Now, that oversight felt like a grave mistake.

"We can ask this new guy, if we're so

concerned." Ryklin's voice was firm. "One of our comrades needs help, and he's going to show up here soon. We help him. Whoever he is."

There was no argument. We'd all survived being cast out from the Legion. We couldn't leave another soldier adrift.

24
KYRIC

LIGHT IN THE DARKNESS.

I wasn't dead.

A figure standing over me.

It all came in flashes, hands helping me out of a shipping crate, my body shivering, suddenly overcome by cold. The contents of my stomach roiling and coming up when I tried to drink the cool water someone handed me.

I wasn't in the Legion anymore.

Death.

I recalled the sentence with cool detachment, the memory as sharp and clear as if it had happened moments ago. The tribunal's split vote echoed in my mind—two to one.

It was the soulless representative who had voted

to spare me. The other two, their faces stern and unforgiving, had sealed my fate with a swift word.

My life came back in a rush, everything that had led me to this moment. Flashes of images as if I was looking at them down a narrow tunnel. No sound. No emotion. Nothing but data.

"Kyric?" One of the men helping me said my name.

I had to blink several times before my vision cleared enough to fully make them out. The room around us was dim, some sort of storage area. And the air smelled too recycled to be anywhere but a space station.

"Drex. Zyrus." I recognized them both. Two men I'd saved before I became soulless, before I stopped being able to save anyone.

I tried to step forward, but my knee went out from under me, and Zyrus held me up, wedging himself under my armpit.

"He needs a medic," said Zyrus.

"You were all like this. We have the medscanner back in the room. Let's get him out of here before someone catches us."

And they led me down an unfamiliar hallway, leaving me to wonder what I was supposed to do next.

25
ASTRID

THE WOMAN from station security came through. I still didn't know her name, and I hadn't seen her since she helped us save Alice. But I was sitting in front of a special arrival bay with a scowling Commander Henner speaking on the comm to the ship that was only a few minutes away.

I squeezed Zyrus's hand, feeling the warmth of his skin against mine. A pang of longing hit me as I thought of our absent friend. "I wish Alice was here to see this," I murmured, my eyes fixed on the arrival bay.

Zyrus's deep voice rumbled beside me. "I'm sure she's happy to be heading towards her family." His words were reassuring.

"I hope so." But I couldn't imagine leaving the

station without saying goodbye to the people I'd spent the last ten years surviving with.

There was a rumble, and the outer doors of the station shuddered and opened, revealing a ground transport ship hovering outside the entrance. It slowly inched forward until the doors closed behind it, and its landing gears came out before it set down.

My people were finally home.

Or, well, not home, exactly, but no longer stranded without hope of escape.

A med team hustled towards the cargo bay door, their equipment clattering as they rushed inside the transport. The minutes dragged on, each second feeling like an eternity as we waited for any sign of movement. Even the station security crew who had run this retrieval mission remained out of sight.

My heart pounded, and I found myself holding my breath, straining to catch any sound or glimpse of what was happening within the ship. The air felt thick with tension, and I could sense Zyrus shifting uneasily beside me.

And then Maddie and her parents stepped off the ship, and I could finally take a deep breath. Maddie was nine years old, one of the first kids born in our little settlement. And if there was ever a child with a hundred parents, it was her.

Then there was Solara. Galen. Kai. Rook and his family. I counted them all off in my head, a mental census to ensure that everyone really was there.

Davis was the last off the ship, limping and leaning on a cane made from a sturdy branch. That was new.

Zyrus squeezed my hand one last time before releasing it. I sprang into action, my heart racing as I darted past the handful of station security personnel who stood at attention, their presence more for show than necessity.

Ignoring their watchful eyes, I pushed through the secure door. The metallic hiss of the door closing behind me barely registered as I sprinted towards my people, my feet carrying me faster than I thought possible. The familiar faces before me blurred as tears of relief welled in my eyes, threatening to spill over at any moment.

A whoop of joy pierced the air, echoing through the arrival bay. I couldn't pinpoint its source, but it sparked a chain reaction of elation among the reunited group.

Before I knew it, arms enveloped me from all directions. The embrace felt like it came from a hundred people at once, their warmth and relief palpable. Tears flowed freely, mingling with laughter and exclamations of disbelief. The emotional whirlwind swept us up, blending joy at our reunion with the raw ache of loss for those who didn't survive. Amid the chaos of hugs and tearful greetings, I caught glimpses of hope in their eyes—a tentative optimism for what lay ahead. The cacophony of voices and sensations overwhelmed me, yet I clung to each moment, imprinting every detail in my memory.

It was all there in a miasma of people who had once lost everything and now had a chance at going home.

We were herded farther into the station so the crew could clear the transport ship, and I finally made my way to Davis. "How'd that happen?"

He narrowed his eyes and scowled. "Rabbit hole."

I had to bite my lip to keep from laughing. "You're supposed to look where you step."

"A few weeks on this station and you've gone soft." Then we were both smiling and hugging, and the years of strife fell away for at least a little while.

A few crew members were waving the survivors forward and taking down names as well as handing out rooming assignments.

"They've cleaned up Sector J for you," I told

Davis, trying to keep any thoughts of Vastrien or what happened there off my face. "Plenty of space, plenty of warm water and food you don't have to kill yourself. It took Alice a bit to get in touch with her people, but I'm thinking things will get a little easier now."

"They stranded us down there for an extra month. What makes you so optimistic?"

I shrugged. "Sometimes things do go right."

He didn't look convinced.

I spent hours talking to whoever I could, catching up on what had happened since I left, assuring people that Alice was alright, and explaining the room situation.

I had missed this.

I'd been a leader on Nebula, someone my people came to when they needed help. It mostly meant putting out fires—sometimes literally—but it also meant making sure our meals were prepared, that people were doing jobs they were suited for, that we were patrolling our territory to keep the smugglers away. I'd been so busy down there that I almost hadn't had time to feel a decade passing.

Things were different now, but I wasn't going to give this up.

And as I talked and laughed and grieved with my

people, I made a vow to myself that I would make sure everyone got what they needed. Whether that was a ride off of this station to a family back home or a job here so they could stay or anything else that we could dream up together.

We were together again, and anything was possible.

And then there was my mate.

He'd wandered off. After several hours of reacquainting myself with my people, catching up on their struggles and triumphs, I finally broke away from the crowd. My feet carried me back to my quarters, where I found Zyrus hunched over a tablet, his fingers tapping rhythmically on the screen.

The soft glow illuminated his face, highlighting the intense concentration in his eyes. More reflex-building games, I assumed, watching him for a moment. Reflex building games, he called them. But I recognized the furrowed brow of a man trying for a high score.

After another moment, he looked up. "You're back." He said it with a smile. Those smiles were still rare, a precious gift. I hoped I would see more of them, the longer we were together. I'd savor every one.

"I'm back. Everyone's getting settled. And

they're all exhausted. I have a feeling almost everyone is going to fall asleep as soon as they get to their quarters. But I'll be busy helping them soon enough." It was a warning. I wasn't going to ask permission, but I didn't want my mate to think I was ignoring him.

He rose from his seat and drew me into his arms, his warmth enveloping me. The familiar scent of him—a mix of metal and something uniquely alien —filled my senses. "You have your responsibilities," he murmured, his breath tickling my ear. "And I have mine. I wouldn't expect any less from you."

I leaned into him for a moment, savoring the brief respite before duty called again. Then I pulled back slightly, meeting his gaze. "Speaking of your responsibilities ..." I trailed off, thinking of what he'd told me about Kyric, the new Detyen who'd arrived on the station just two days ago. The situation with the newcomer had been weighing on my mind, another potential complication in our already complex lives.

"He's still not talking. Drex says everyone's like this in their first days, but I don't remember. Was I really like that?"

I reached up and traced my finger over his cheekbone, cupping his face. The warmth of his skin seeped into my palm, a reminder of how close we'd come to losing this. "It meant that you survived long enough to find me," I said, my voice barely above a whisper. The weight of those years apart hung between us, but I pushed it aside. "I can never be sorry for that. Not when it brought us here, together." My heart raced, the urgency of our connection thrumming through my veins. We'd overcome so much, and I was determined to face whatever came next, side by side.

His lips crashed against mine, and I surrendered to the kiss, my body melting into his embrace. When he lifted me up, I clung to him, my arms wrapping tightly around his neck. My fingers traced the contours of his muscular shoulders, marveling that this incredible creature was all mine. The heat of his skin seeped through our clothes, igniting a fire within me. As we broke apart for air, I gazed into his eyes, now tinged with red, a testament to the intensity of his emotions. My heart raced, and I knew that no matter what challenges lay ahead, we would face them together.

"I love you, Astrid." His voice was soft, as though he feared the words might spook if he said them too loud.

"I love you too."

I kissed him again. Without fear. Full of hope. Certain, finally, that this was exactly where I belonged.

Thank you for reading Wayward Bond!
I'd appreciate it so much if you would consider leaving a review.

The Detyen Warrior Outcasts series will continue.

NEED A BIT MORE OF WAYWARD BOND?

Sign up at the link below to **receive a free bonus epilogue!**

Find out now!
https://katerudolph.net/index.php/intrepid-bond-bonus/

Looking for EVEN MORE alien romance?
Prince Crux is in a bind.

When the Dragon King commands Crux find a mate, his days of carefree bachelorhood are over.

One trip to a psychic matchmaker and he's on the path to his destiny. But it all comes screeching to a halt when he meets a human woman who lights his inner fire and makes him yearn.

She's got a pair of roller skates and an attitude.

Courtney is supposed to be putting the shambles of her life back together. Getting abducted by aliens isn't part of the plan. Neither is getting rescued by a scorchingly hot dragon that makes her think of an impossible future. But they have no chance together if they can't first escape a planet full of monsters intent on their destruction.

Get your copy of Crux
https://shop.katerudolph.net/products/crux

PREVIEW CRUX

Courtney Lamb's feet were heavy, and she had the headache to end all headaches. She curled into herself on one side, trying to scrunch up into a ball, but her feet dragged along the floor and noise echoed off the metal walls around her.

She was still wearing her roller skates.

How? She always took them off before leaving work. She couldn't exactly drive with wheels on her feet. And yet, as she turned over and pulled her legs in, they slipped on the cold metal floor.

Where was she? This wasn't the root beer stand she worked at, nor was it the creepy, decrepit steel barn that sat on the very edge of the restaurant property. She looked around, squinting in the dim light and trying to get her bearings.

It was industrial, but the room was small. Steel walls. No windows. And a weird echo-y noise in the distance that might have been an air conditioner.

She didn't see a door.

Courtney scrambled to her knees before realizing she wasn't going to get far with roller skates on her feet. She shucked the skates off and wiggled her toes in her sweaty socks before tying the laces together. No matter what was going on, she didn't want to lose her skates.

They were expensive. And one of the few nice things she had left.

There was a shriek down the hall, or at least, Courtney assumed there was a hall, and she flinched.

What the hell was going on?

Had she been kidnapped? Was she being trafficked? She'd seen plenty of Facebook posts talking about the perils of being a woman in America, but most of it seemed like a bunch of bullshit. People didn't *actually* hide under cars to slit the Achilles tendons of the unsuspecting.

Right?

She ran a hand down the back of her leg, as if to assure herself that she was intact. Obviously she was. Other than the headache, she wasn't hurt.

She was just confused.

And in trouble.

She wanted to call for help, but a second scream from somewhere in the building made her throat freeze up. No, she didn't want to call attention to herself.

With her skate laces tied together, she was able to sling her skates over her shoulder and get to her feet. The room seemed even tinier when she was standing up. Was she a prisoner? Why?

Her mom was going to kill her when she found out.

Of course, Courtney hadn't spoken to her mother in months, and now was not the time to think about how this would impact her mother's career. She was in the middle of an abduction, she had to care about herself.

She stroked the top of her skate, half for comfort, half to remind herself that it was sturdy and could probably be used as some kind of weapon.

She was wearing the thick leggings and short sleeve red tunic that made up her work uniform, though her name badge must have fallen off some-where. That furthered Courtney's theory that she'd been taken from work.

She couldn't remember clocking out. She

wracked her brain, but the last thing she remembered was telling her co-worker, Sarah, that she didn't have any plans for the weekend. The same as every weekend these days.

That wasn't what she should be feeling bad about at the moment.

Was Sarah a trafficker? Had she waited to strike until Courtney was at her most vulnerable?

No. That was ridiculous. Sarah was a college student trying to make ends meet. She wasn't sinister.

Where was the freaking door?

Courtney whirled around, but she still didn't see anything that looked like it would let her out of the room. She was in a metal tomb and she couldn't escape.

Her breaths came faster and faster, and black spots danced in front of her eyes.

No. No. Now was not the time for a panic attack.

She hadn't had one in months, and she didn't want them to restart. They sucked.

And so did her whole situation.

"Think of the good things," she commanded herself. There weren't many. But she had to number them off. "I'm in my regular clothes. My skates are fine. I'm not hurt." She ran out of optimism after that. Any other "good" news sounded like asking for trouble, and Courtney wasn't interested in that.

She ran her hands over the metal walls, looking for a seam that might reveal a hidden door. There had to be something. She had been put in the room, so there had to be a way to get her out of it. She looked up, wondering if she'd somehow been lowered in, but the ceiling was too high to make out any fine detail in the dim light.

Where was the light even coming from?

There wasn't a ceiling light. She didn't see lights in the floor. There was just a faint, pale blue glow all around her that allowed her to see.

It was another good thing, and Courtney decided not to question it.

She had her skates, but she wished she had a skate tool. That fancy little wrench might have helped her pry an invisible door open. But her skate tool and spare wheels were in her bag at work. Along with her cell phone, a bit of cash, and her car keys. She had no way to contact anyone for help.

And *there* was the hyperventilation.

She tried to control her breathing, but the walls felt like they were closing in. She heard footsteps coming her way and shrank back as far away from the sound as she could. The room was maybe six feet wide. She couldn't shrink back much.

A brave woman would have done something. Courtney *wished* she was brave. But she couldn't think and she wanted to live. She was pretty sure brave people died quicker than cowards.

The wall opposite her glowed a faint yellow, and a rectangle formed before sliding to one side, the invisible door revealing itself. A brave woman would have charged.

Instead, Courtney watched a monster step inside.

It—and it was clearly an *it*, not a person—was some kind of *creature*. Over eight feet tall, antennae coming out of its head, and sinister purple skin that was covered in a faint slime. It wore clothes over most of its body, but its arms were exposed, and scars or tattoos or something covered it.

One of its hands wasn't a hand at all. Instead, it came to a fine point and had an edge that made it look like a sword.

It looked like something out of *Star Trek*.

And she was wearing a red shirt.

Shit.

It wore pants, but judging by the giant bulge right where his dick should be, he didn't plan on wearing them for long. And she didn't want to find out if his dick was a knife too.

Working by instinct, not pausing to think, Courtney grabbed onto one of her skates and swung, sending the other one flying at the monster's head. He didn't expect it, and the wheels, metal plate, and carbon fiber boot were enough to send him slumping to the ground.

Oh god, was he dead? Had she broken her skate?

Courtney flailed for a moment and cut off the horrible noise that tried to escape her throat. She checked her skate first. Except for a bit of slime and something that might have been monster blood, it seemed fine.

Good.

She didn't know how to check for a pulse on a monster. She didn't know if she wanted him to be dead or alive.

Oh god. What was she going to do?

She had to run.

She stepped around the monster and dove through the door, just in case it tried to close. The hallway was narrow and lit up by the same ambient blue light as her cell. She chose a direction and ran, unsure if it was correct but refusing to hesitate.

She stumbled when she passed a window.

Courtney came to a halt and looked outside.

She expected a city. Maybe some trees. *Something*.

Instead, she saw the black of space.

Outer space.

She wasn't in a warehouse. She was on a space ship, and they were hovering above some planet that didn't look like Earth.

How was she going to get home?

She was trying to think, then something impacted the ship, and Courtney stumbled as the lights went out and all of her senses went haywire.

ALSO BY KATE RUDOLPH

Detyen Warrior Outcasts
Fated Mate Alien Romance
These doomed warriors were abandoned by their
people and live on the edge. Their mates hold the
key to their salvation.
Pick a book and jump into the action today!

Dangerous Bond
Intrepid Bond
Wayward Bond

Mated to the Alien
Fated Mate Alien Romance

Detyens are doomed to die young if they don't find their fated mates.

Follow along as these mated pairs fight off aliens, corrupt dictators, prejudiced humans, pirates, and more! The books can be read or listened to in any order, though some characters show up in multiple stories.

Select books available in audio.

Pick a book and jump into the action today!

Ruwen

Tyral

Stoan

Cyborg

Krayter

Kayleb

Shayn

Braxtyn

Doryan

Dekon

Detyen Warriors
Detya was destroyed a hundred years ago. These doomed warriors are out to find justice... and their mates.

The Detyen Warriors series brings you kick butt heroines, alpha alien heroes, fated mates, and relationships strong enough to span the galaxy! **The entire series is also available in audio!**

Soulless

Ruthless

Heartless

Faultless

Endless

Guarded by the Shifter

Werewolf. Bodyguard. Mate.
The origins of these shifters are shrouded in mystery, but they're determined to protect their mates from any harm that comes their way.
Also available in audio!

Hunting Season

On the Prowl

Stalking Magic

Wolf Cursed

Hungry for the Wolf

Wolf's Temptation

Stealing the Alpha

The thief takes what she wants, but the alpha keeps what's his...

Join shifter thief Mel as she clashes with lion alpha Luke in an explosive trilogy of two opposites who can't keep away from one another.

Also available in audio!

The Alpha Heist
Entangled with the Thief
In the Alpha's Bed

Alien Mates: Planet Exile

Guerran is no place for pretty human women. But these alien heroes will protect their mates!

Also available in audio!

Exile's Hunter
Exile's Adored

Zulir Warrior Mates

Kidnapped humans. Alien Warriors. Electric wings.

The Zulir Warrior Mates series brings you human heroines and heroes abducted from Earth who find love – and wings! – with the alien warriors who rescue them.

Also available in audio!

Synnr's Saint

Synnr's Hope

Synnr's Spark

Synnr's Kiss

Synnr's Ride

Dragon Brides

Dragon Princes. Fierce Women. Love.

Fated mates, fierce women, and dragon princes are ready to find their mates.

Crux

Ranger

Saber

Cipher

Storm

Drake

Asher

Knox

Flint

Alien Holiday Romance

Christmas... in space????
These alien holiday romances look beyond Earth's winter holidays and ring in the season across the galaxy!
Select titles available in audio.
Snowed in with the Alien Beast
The Alien's Winter Gift
The Alien Reindeer's Wild Ride
Trapped with her Alien Mate

Alien Outlaws

Outlaws, schemes, and love... it's all there in the Alien Outlaws series...

Andie Munster is sick of life on Ixilta, the planet she got dumped on after being abducted from Earth six years ago. And when the mysterious and dangerous Xandr shows up looking for a way off the planet, she's half-prisoner, half-co-conspirator in a wild rush to escape.

Rogue Alien's Escape

Rogue Alien's Woman

Rogue Alien's Secret

Rogue Alien's Legacy

Find more by Kate Rudolph at www. katerudolph.net

ABOUT KATE RUDOLPH

KATE RUDOLPH IS a paranormal and sci-fi romance writer who lives in Indiana. She loves writing about kick butt heroines and the steamy heroes who love them. She's been devouring romance novels since she was too young to be reading them and had to hide her books so no one would take them away. She couldn't imagine a better job in this world than writing romances and sharing them with her fellow readers.

If you enjoyed this story, please consider leaving a review.